She ran a male prostitution ring!

What a perfect racket for the mayor's daughter, Chance thought. She almost had the perfect crime going. Ingenious. Only she hadn't counted on Chance McCoy coming to town.

"I'm sorry," Hannah whispered.

He pierced her with his most daunting stare. She didn't flinch. Sure she was sorry. She knew her whole operation was about to go down. Her Hunk-toys would be history. Like the infamous La Grange, Texas, Chicken Ranch. The one they made into that play, *The Best Little Whorehouse in Texas.*

"Let me make it up to you," Hannah said brightly, obviously trying to lighten the mood. "How would you like to go to a party with me tonight?"

"The Hunk party?" he asked sarcastically, taking Hannah's business card out of his pocket. "Hannah's Hunks—We Cater to Your Every Need," he read.

"Oh!" Her eyes lit up in recognition. "All right, I admit it," she said, leading him into the house. "Really, you're so quick. Intelligent. And a Yankee, to boot. I'm so impressed." Once they got into the kitchen, the scent of rum and chocolate overwhelmed him.

"Don't stand there sniffing. I want you to sample what's made me so famous around town," Hannah said, holding out a small, semi-round, squished-up brown ball. "My Hunks."

Dear Reader,

Spring is the season for love! LOVE & LAUGHTER celebrates with another month of romantic comedies that tickle the funny bone and reveal more than a few truths about falling in love!

Our Matchmaking Moms (from Hell) miniseries continues with *One Mom Too Many* by always popular and talented Vicki Lewis Thompson. This delightful tale has two moms with marriage on their minds—for their kids. Little do they suspect they have done their work too well....

We also welcome another new author, Bonnie Tucker, to LOVE & LAUGHTER. In *Hannah's Hunks* the heroine, Hannah, is a caterer who can't find her way around a kitchen, but cooks up a mess of trouble when she runs into undercover agent Chance McCoy. He's investigating everyone in the small, serene town of Sugar Land, most especially the beautiful caterer who can't cook and seems to be running an undercover operation of her own.

Have a few laughs on us!

Malle Vallik

Malle Vallik
Associate Senior Editor

HANNAH'S HUNKS
Bonnie Tucker

Harlequin Books

TORONTO • NEW YORK • LONDON
AMSTERDAM • PARIS • SYDNEY • HAMBURG
STOCKHOLM • ATHENS • TOKYO • MILAN
MADRID • WARSAW • BUDAPEST • AUCKLAND

ISBN 0-373-44018-9

HANNAH'S HUNKS

Printed in U.S.A.

"I live in a small town outside a big city with my husband, three kids, three dogs, four cats, five guinea pigs, fish, turtles and a bird," says new author **Bonnie Tucker.** "All I have to do is get up in the morning and my day is a story waiting to be written. In fact, the idea for *Hannah's Hunks* came to me when I made my son a pumpkin cake for his birthday. For some reason, the cake plotzed. *Hannah's Hunks* is a fictional story, but the scene about the pumpkin cake really *did* happen, right down to every last substituted ingredient, including the pancake mix. I still say the cake should have come out perfectly. But then again, if it had, I might not have written this book."

P.S. Bonnie would love to hear from her readers. You can write to her at: P.O. Box 5009-572
Sugar Land, TX 77487

Special thanks to:
DebbiQ, JanF, JolieK, KathyMP, and KimR

For their patience and expertise: Vicki Lemonds,
Roxanne Rustand, Jim Crider and Kathleen McKeague

With love to: Ed, Elizabeth, Eric, Jessica,
Beverly, Herman, and Mike

And to my editor, Brenda Chin, who made all my
wishes come true—only better

HANNAH'S HUNKS
BOURBON BALLS

1 6-oz package of chocolate chips
2 tbs Karo syrup
1/2 cup bourbon*
1 cup chopped nuts
2 1/2 cups crushed vanilla wafers
powdered sugar**

Melt chocolate chips over hot water.
Mix Karo syrup and bourbon well and add to
melted chocolate.
Add nuts and crushed vanilla wafers. Mix well.
Let stand for 20 minutes. Form into balls and roll
in powdered sugar.**

* Hannah substituted rum for bourbon.
**Hannah didn't use the powdered sugar.

Enjoy!

1

HANNAH HART'S FINGERS grasped the brass doorknob with a crushing hold. Her gaze flickered over the Ada Hart, Mayor nameplate, then focused out the window behind the receptionist's desk into the parking lot two stories below.

To anyone else it would seem to be an ordinary parking lot, surfaced in gray concrete and painted with white lines. Parked on the lot were ordinary vehicles of various shapes, sizes and ages.

What made this particular parking lot worth Hannah's interest, though, was one little red car. One very sad, little red car, in the second row, six spaces over.

"It's not as if I did it on purpose," Hannah murmured. "Backing up gets me all the time."

Squaring her shoulders, she turned the knob and opened the door. She knew what to expect. Ada's special brand of maternal guilt. No one did it better than her mother.

Bright morning sunlight greeted her, pouring in through the floor-to-ceiling windows, powerful enough to make the dust motes dance. Her mother stood in front of the glass, cutting Hannah's view of the parking lot in half.

Hannah walked slowly toward her mother, when the man sitting in the leather chair in front of Ada's desk turned. Hannah's step faltered. He slowly stood, and she stopped breathing.

It was at that exact moment, Hannah knew without a doubt that for all the things she had ever done wrong in her life, she must have done something exceedingly right. Because here, standing in front of her, was the prize.

To call him handsome would be an understatement. This man was the most salacious mass of meaty muscle she'd ever had the pleasure to share space with. He reeked of untamed sexuality. She could smell it on him, blatant and undulating.

And he did something to her insides, which must have loosened her pulmonary veins, because as soon as he took a step toward her, her heart flipped over six times in her chest.

How could it not? He tugged at the knot on his burgundy club tie, pinned her with his dark brown eyes, raised one eyebrow, then gave her a look that said, "I know your heart flipped six times, and babe, I can make it seven."

She almost had to sigh out loud, just to release the burgeoning desire inside her.

He wore his dark hair long, slightly over the collar. One piece had strayed down toward his left eyebrow, and she wanted so much to go over to him and brush it back. Then she'd rub her breasts against his chest as if she were a cat and he were the couch, and finally rip his clothes off and have her way with him. She practically wept with wanting.

Only she didn't. Because she was dignified and shy, and her mother watched.

Her mother. How could she have forgotten? Hannah turned her attention toward the stately woman with the perfectly coiffed, light red hair, who had her arms crossed over her stately white suit, as she drummed her manicured fingertips on her stately sleeve, all the while watching her daughter with very stately amusement. The mayor would never ogle a man. Not only would it show bad taste, it wouldn't be stately.

"You're late, dear," Ada's cultivated voice suggested only the hint of a Southern drawl.

Hannah drifted past the man, through a mist of invisible heat radiating from his body, and over to her mother. She brushed Ada's cheek with a kiss and whispered, "It couldn't be helped." Hannah shifted her gaze out the window, found the little red Mustang with the realigned front end, and hoped, when her mother saw the car, she'd remember they were related by blood.

Ada followed the direction of Hannah's stare. And Hannah knew the exact moment her mother saw the smashed car, because she squeezed Hannah's arm until those stately fingernails dug all the way through the material of Hannah's jacket and found skin. Then her mother sharply whispered, as only she could do, in a very refined, very mayoral voice, "Again."

Hannah nodded.

Ada had always been known for her intuitive mind. It was no wonder she'd been elected mayor for the past three terms. Hannah had no doubt the upcoming election would bring another victory. Not one to mince words, Ada breathed in Hannah's ear, "How could you?"

Hannah really didn't know how it could have happened again. "It was an accident."

"Can I help with something?" the hunk to die for asked, his deep voice filling all the empty spaces in the room, surrounding her, caressing her.

Hannah wondered if maybe she should give him a shovel and let him go outside and dig a hole for her to crawl into. It wouldn't be a bad punishment, if he'd take off his shirt while digging. She could watch his chest glisten in the sun and his muscles expand and contract as he labored. She'd bet her next car-insurance payment, if it wasn't canceled, that under his sport coat he had bulging biceps. Would it be too much to ask if she could watch his biceps bulge and his chest glisten? Absolutely not. After all, even she deserved something to take her mind off of everything that had gone wrong today.

So naturally she said, "Yes."

"No," Ada answered at the same time, sending Hannah a censuring look.

He chuckled. Hannah didn't miss the knowing gleam in his eye, and hoped the brain behind those brown eyes of his didn't know she'd been thinking about all his very correct anatomical attributes. After all, she knew—as did every other woman in Sugar Land—that men didn't date women with scientific minds.

"So this is the daughter you've been telling me about." Mr. Majestic walked around Ada's desk until he stood directly in front of Hannah. He extended his hand, waiting.

She stared down at his fingers and opened her mouth a tiny bit. She wanted to say something witty, only the words were stuck in her throat somewhere and wouldn't come out.

"She certainly is." Ada didn't sound too pleased and gave Hannah a slight nudge in the back, which was enough to get her moving again. "Dear." The endearment sounded painful. "Meet Chance McCoy. He's taking over the job as Sugar Land parks-and-recreation director while Gus Rappaport's on paternity leave."

The man captured Hannah's hand and shook firmly. She held back a sigh of contentment when warm, slightly rough skin met her soft palm. He didn't hold on any longer than proper, but somehow even after he let her hand go she felt as if they still touched.

"Sugar Land's certainly glad you can fill in for Gus while he's at home helping his wife and baby." She didn't recognize the husky breathiness of her voice and quickly cleared her throat.

"It's very nineties for this small town to provide a paternity leave for fathers."

"Isn't it, though? We even have maternity leave for mothers."

"I'm impressed," he said seriously.

"Thank you, Mr. McCoy."

"It's Chance."

This time she looked directly into his coffee—with a little bit of cream, if you please—colored eyes and when his gaze collided with hers, she wondered if he had felt the bang, too.

"Yes, it's a chance, but we all take chances. I'm sure other small cities give their employees similar benefits."

"The name."

"What name?"

"Mine. It's Chance."

"Of course, it is. I knew that." Could this day get any worse?

Maybe. Still, there were a few good points. Like now, when his gaze traveled slowly down her neck, her breasts, her hips, thighs and shoes, then took its time to head back up again. Everywhere his glance touched, she tingled. She was so glad she had worn her very severe navy blue suit instead of the St. John knit. Not that the St. John was anything other than classic, but under his scrutiny he made her feel as if she were standing there naked. And she'd much rather be imagined naked covered in a three-piece suit, than in a clingy oyster-pink knit.

"Sit down, both of you." Ada's no-nonsense tone brought her back to earth.

Hannah settled in the burgundy chair next to Chance's and asked, "Which part of Texas are you from? I don't recognize your accent." The little red car she'd hit had Virginia plates.

"I grew up in Chicago."

"A Yankee." She breathed a sigh of relief.

"I haven't been back in a long time."

Hannah felt it coming, all the way down to the middle of her bones, before he even said the words. She pictured herself as Marie Antoinette walking up to the guillotine, bending over, neck placed in the half-moon notch, saying her last words, *"Pardon, monsieur. I did not do it on purpose."* She clutched her purse, tossed her head so her hair flipped over her shoulder and tried not to squirm. "Really. Where have you been living more recently?"

"Virginia."

The blade fell.

"Oh." Her hand jerked to the back of her neck, feeling for the wound. "What a lovely place."

What else could she say? She didn't think this would be a good time to tell him his old red Mustang had received a slight cosmetic makeover within the past few minutes. And she knew it had to be his, since no one else living in Sugar Land had Virginia plates. So much for thoughts of glistening chests and panting biceps. Or even the glimmer of hope that maybe they would make mad, passionate love on a rope hammock. When this guy went outside and saw his car he was going to hunt her down, and it wouldn't be for sex. Not that she would have consented anyway—she didn't even own a hammock—but still, it would have been nice to dream about it. To have been asked about it. To have had the opportunity to say no. And now even those dreams were dashed.

Chance watched Hannah mold herself primly to the chair. She kept her back rigid, eyes straight ahead and knees glued together, crossing those long, long legs at very trim ankles. She must have smoothed down that skirt for about the hundredth time before finally giving it a rest and folding her hands serenely on top of her leather purse.

Three days earlier, Jim Mitchell, his boss at the agency, had given him the bad news. His Cancún vacation was being canceled for the fourth time in less than a year. No sun. No margaritas. No topless women calling out to him. Instead, he'd been ordered to Sugar Land.

Jim and Sugar Land's police chief, Clayton Turley, had grown up together, enlisted in the army together and served in 'Nam side by side. When Turley discovered Sugar Land was being used as the southwest distribution center for heroin, he had turned to Jim for help.

Chance knew he was the best agent in the organization, but still, going undercover as a parks director was pushing even his talents a little too far. He'd choke on pollution-free air. Give him some good, old smog and lots of concrete, and he was in his element.

Chance figured that once his sixth sense, those uncanny hunches he had been born with, kicked in, he should be able to zero in on whoever was behind the drug ring and have them arrested within a week. Sugar Land should be a piece of cake.

And those hunches were working like a charm. Right now, as he sat next to sweet Hannah, he could sense she was a pure, innocent woman who probably never jay-walked, swore or had ever been given so much as a parking ticket.

One look at her and he knew all there was to know. She had V-I-R-G-I-N written across her chest as clearly as if she were Hester Prynne wearing a scarlet letter. All she needed was a pair of white gloves and a Peter Pan collar for the picture to be complete.

Sex, he could tell, was something this lady never

thought about. What a shame. She had potential. Her pouty, full lips were made for kissing. And he'd love to see her large golden eyes burn with passion. For him.

If anything could cause him to lose control, and Chance prided himself on never losing control, it would be that hair. Fiery auburn, curling down her back. Or better yet, spread across his pillow. Chance wanted Hannah to read the desire in his eyes, to let her know, without saying the words, that he'd be available while in town.

But, right now, her mother watched, and he didn't think Ada would appreciate the thoughts he entertained about her daughter. Anyway, the object of his fantasy wasn't paying any attention to him. She stared out the window and he couldn't figure out why a parking lot would hold her interest more than he did. And that irked.

Ada looked from Hannah to him, back to Hannah again and said, "I bet you didn't know Chance drove all the way here from Virginia?"

"I bet I could have guessed," she replied almost sarcastically, while at the same time sending him a warm smile. A heated smile.

"You really should have flown in," Ada said. "Weren't you advised we'd ship the car for you?"

He dragged his gaze away from Hannah's lips and made himself concentrate on the mayor. "The car's been in storage for the winter months." On his last assignment, he'd gone undercover as a homeless man in Harlem. He had lived on the streets, sleeping in doorways some nights and vacant, rat-infested apartments others. "I enjoy the freedom of the road and the drive here was cathartic." Considering the life he led was full of half-truths and outright fabrications, this was the most honest statement he could ever make. "My car's special to me."

"Yes, well. That's nice." Ada stared at Hannah.

Chance felt silent signals zing between the two women like a charged lightning rod. Then Ada sent Hannah *the look*. Normally he could read all kinds of looks people passed back and forth. But not this one. He figured it must be a mother-daughter look thing, so powerful not even his sixth sense could pick up on the meaning.

"I wouldn't have had the car shipped anyway," Chance said, his glance first stopping at Ada, then lingering on Hannah's flushed face. She had settled herself deeper in the chair. Her breasts rose and fell in a mesmerizing rhythm that a lesser man would find hypnotic. Good thing he wasn't a lesser man. However, he was still a man with a capital *M*, who hadn't slept in thirty-six hours. So he forced his gaze away from Hannah's mesmerizing, hypnotizing breasts and said to Ada, "I always avoid taking risks with my Mustang. Shipping companies don't care if they dent or scratch a car."

Now, both women listened intently to every word he said. He liked the way these Texas women paid attention. Nothing in the dossier he'd been given about Sugar Land, this assignment or the parks-director role he would play while here had mentioned anything about that. "My Mustang's a classic," he added to impress the younger Ms. Hart.

"A classic. Well, isn't that something, Mother?" Instead of looking impressed, her top front teeth bit into the side of her lower lip.

"Yes, something." Ada glared at her daughter before smiling sweetly at him. "I'm sure it was—is. Classic, that is."

Chance felt those unreadable signals passing between them again. The force field—heavily loaded.

Ada cleared her throat and straightened a stack of papers on her desk. Three times. "Time to get back to business.

There's a problem with the house my secretary rented for you."

"Problem?" He didn't need problems. What he needed was a hot shower, a cold beer and a bed.

"It burned to the ground three days ago."

He leaned forward, his fists clenched, exhaustion taking over where adrenaline had been. "I'm assuming you have an alternative."

"I'm the mayor, Mr. McCoy. I always have alternatives. In fact, that's why I asked Hannah to come over to my office this morning to meet you. I would like you to move into her garage apartment."

"Mother." Hannah clipped out the word as if it were blasphemous. Red heat streaked up her neck. "I rushed all the way over here because you want me to lease him the garage apartment?" She tossed her head in the direction of the window. "This was the emergency you called me about? The thing you told me to get right over here and make sure I wore lipstick about?"

"It seemed important at the time, dear."

"If you had told me what you wanted on the phone instead of ordering me to *speed* over here, and you know how nervous I get when I'm in a *hurry,* I could have told you my answer an hour ago." Hannah turned to face him. "No."

"Totally unacceptable. Think again," Ada ordered.

Hannah ignored Ada and spoke directly to Chance. "I've been running an ad in the paper and several people have called."

"You've been running that ad for six months now and haven't had a nibble. You have a live one right here. Snap him up."

"Well, now you've heard the truth. No one else is interested, so I doubt you will be, either."

"I'm sure he'll be interested." Ada's smile didn't reach her eyes. "The reason I asked Hannah to rush on over here was so she could see if you'd do."

"If I'd do?" He looked over at Miss Prim and Proper and schooled his face into a bland mask. Chance McCoy not only would *do,* he had always been requested. Even demanded, on more than one occasion.

"Now that I've met him, I can see he won't do at all."

Won't do? No proper little miss sitting in her chair looking like some overage schoolgirl—make that overage, virginal schoolgirl—was going to tell him he wouldn't "do."

"Han-nah." Ada clearly sent a warning. "Houses don't come available for lease in town every day, dear. You don't have a choice. You'll have to make *do.*"

Hannah ignored her mother and gave him her full attention and a very apologetic smile. "It's not that I have any objection to renting the apartment to you. But my mother's right. I've been running the ad for a long time, and it's very difficult to find the perfect tenant. Don't you think matching an apartment to a tenant is like choosing a husband for a wife? You have to find the perfect match. This apartment is small and I don't think you'd suit each other. No. No, I've made up my mind. You won't *do,* at all."

Hannah swept her gaze over his long legs, his bulging thigh muscles, and other bulges only hinted at underneath his jeans—and knew he'd do only too well.

"All I need is a bed." He sent her a knowing grin. "Any bed, even a small one, in a small apartment, will *do* fine."

Hannah wanted nothing more than to kiss that grin off his too handsome face. Instead, she said, "You just won't do, at all."

She risked a glance at her mother, who looked back at her as if she thought her crazy. Hannah lifted her chin higher and refolded her hands. She refused to surrender under the pressure. She knew what would happen if Chance moved in. He'd learn all her secrets and use them against her, use them to hurt her, just like dumb, dead Dave had. And Dave had been a Yankee, too. She wasn't going to let that happen again. At least, not intentionally.

"Hannah, dear, Chance needs to move in this afternoon. What exactly is the problem?"

"There's no problem. Really." Her mother knew exactly what the problems were, and the biggest one at the moment sat outside in the parking lot. Then, Hannah noticed Ada's teeth. They were clenched together. She'd never seen her mother clench her teeth.

She glanced at Chance. He was too good-looking and he made her juices flow in places they hadn't flowed in a long, long time. She just couldn't rent the place to him. Her heart was too tender, too easily broken. "Your comfort, Mr. McCoy, is all that concerns me."

"All I need is a bed to stretch out on," he said, his voice soft. Seductive. Persuasive. "And a place to lay my boots."

Hannah was hard-pressed not to think of him laid out on her bed, with his boots on and nothing else. She looked down at his feet. He wore white running shoes. End of fantasy.

Beginning of another. "I was raised to believe a man should have his creature comforts." Hannah's mother thought a man nothing more than an obstacle to step over while traveling the road to success. "Men are only good for two things," Ada had preached. "The second being cooking steaks on the outdoor grill."

Hannah glanced out the window again. The red car could be seen by everyone whose window faced this side of the building and she wondered why he didn't notice it.

Well, maybe a parks-and-recreation director didn't look at the world around him if it didn't have an oak tree in there somewhere, and a couple of sparrows, too.

He would find out soon enough, though. He'd go outside when it was time for him to leave, he'd walk up to that old, smashed-up red Mustang, pull her card off the windshield and then know she, Hannah Hart, friend to the world, with the exception of him, had done the damage.

And she'd been worrying about him staying in her garage apartment, and how she would have to resist taking advantage of his muscles and meat once he was there? Hah! She might as well give in to her mother and Chance both. He'd never move in, anyway. Once he saw the car, he'd do whatever he could to stay as far from her as possible, even if it meant sleeping outside on one of his own park benches.

So Hannah did the only thing she could possibly do under the circumstances. She acquiesced. God, sometimes she was such a pushover. Her mother had always said she was a throwback to tainted genes on her father's side. He had a great-grandfather who had been born and raised in California. No one in the family was allowed to talk about him. "You're both absolutely right. And when you're right, you're right." Hannah clasped her hands together, then gifted Chance with the most brilliant smile three years of braces could buy. "I don't know why I'm trying to discourage you. Allow me to give you a proper welcome to Sugar Land and tell you how much I look forward to being neighbors."

Hannah stood and Chance followed. She held out her hand. He engulfed it in his, and this time when he let go he slid his fingers over her palm, sending chills up one arm and down the other. Pity she had such a problem backing up. He had so much potential.

"I'll see you this afternoon, then," he murmured, his voice deep and full of promise.

"I'm sure you will."

Chance watched as Hannah, fiery curls swaying down her backside, left the office without bothering to close the door behind her. Definitely one tight, little package. Even though he never mixed business with pleasure, he could still fantasize about all the possibilities. Maybe when he finished the Sugar Land assignment and finally took his vacation, the delectable Miss Hart might agree to a no-strings-attached weekend in Cancún, where he could show her what a real man was made of.

Chance pulled out a pen and small notebook from the inside pocket of his jacket. He flipped open to a blank page, ready to write down directions to the apartment.

"You're used to working in big cities, like New York, and I'm concerned you won't take our drug problem here in Sugar Land seriously," Ada said.

"I take all drug problems seriously, no matter what the size of the city."

"Maybe you do. Maybe you don't. You know, I wanted to bring in the Texas Rangers. But Clayton insisted on you. And he won."

Ada looked disgusted. Chance kept his expression blank and said nothing. He refused to defend himself to this woman, even if she was the mayor of a city named after a sweetener put in coffee. He had a ninety-nine percent success rate during his ten-year career as an undercover agent. The figures spoke for themselves. Only once had he screwed up. Philadelphia. But Philly would never happen again. Texas Rangers be damned.

After several long minutes, Ada broke the silence. "It's not that I don't like you. I don't know you well enough not to like you. Yet. So believe me when I tell you it's nothing personal. However, I have a policy about hiring locals to work for the city. And since you're from a part of the country that's completely foreign to what Sugar Land, in particular, and Texas, in general, stands for, I know you won't fit in. And then this whole undercover operation you and Clayton have worked out will be for nothing. We'll probably be worse off after you leave. I know we should have called in the Rangers.''

"I'm a chameleon. I fit in everywhere.''

"But not Texas. You speak a different language. You eat different food. You even look different.''

Chance raised an eyebrow. "You don't want me here, and I didn't want to *be* here in the first place. But we're stuck with each other. I was supposed to be off on a two-week vacation in Cancún, but I came here as a favor to your police chief and my boss. Jim sent me because I'm the best man for the job. Where do you think I'd rather be?''

"Between Cancún and Sugar Land? Right here, of course.''

He chuckled. "I don't need my sixth sense to know the reason you were elected mayor.''

"That's another thing I wanted to ask you about. Your sixth sense. Clayton told me all about how you work on hunches. Are they working? Right now?''

"They always work.''

"He said you have the ability to stand anywhere, be anywhere, and those hunches come to you. Like this.'' She snapped her fingers.

"Not quite as fast as that.'' Although he did feel a twinge of something right now. Something he couldn't put his finger on.

Ada went to the window and stared outside. "So if there

was anything wrong—anything, at all—you'd feel it. Is that right?''

"That's how it works."

"Do you feel anything right now?"

"No."

"I didn't think so," she sighed despondently and went back to her desk. "Let me give you directions to Hannah's house."

Moments later, out in the parking lot, Chance stood, staring at the broken glass from the headlights of his tortured cherry-red Mustang. A paralyzing fear churned in his gut. It had been ten years since the Philly incident. Ten years since his instinct had screwed up.

He saw a pink business card peeking at him from underneath the windshield wiper. He reached across the accordion-bent hood, pulled it out and read, "Hannah's Hunks—We Cater to Your Every Need."

Hannah had done this? She had sat right next to him. He had touched her hand. He had breathed the same air she had. And he hadn't a clue.

Philly all over again.

He'd been young, only twenty-two. Working the graveyard shift.

She'd been tall, slender, blond and busty.

He had fallen. Hard and fast. Never even knew his hunches had taken a hike until the night she pulled the gun.

His instincts had left him once upon a time in Philly. He had made a mistake then, and still had the scar to prove it.

But he never made the same mistake twice.

2

EVEN THOUGH HER KITCHEN was toward the back of the house and Brooks and Dunn's "Boot Scootin' Boogie" blared from the stereo speakers, Hannah still heard Chance's car chug down Blossom Trail Drive.

The distinct grinding of metal on metal could only come from a car whose front end had been squished together. And as far as she knew, no one on Blossom Trail Drive owned a car with mangled body parts. At least, not since her neighbor from across the street, Harold, had had the driver's-side door of his Cadillac fixed.

Hannah wrenched the wooden spoon out from the thick batter of Hannah's Hunks' Sweet Chocolate Chunks. Her belly muscles contracted when she heard the car pull up in front of her house. The roaring motor was cut, but not before three loud pops and a long hiss spewed forth. Finally, she heard the car door open with a loud, groaning creak and then slam shut.

The spoon dropped out of her hand, missed the bowl and landed with a thump on the countertop, splattering chocolate and rum.

Hannah swiped the counter with a sponge and washed her hands, wiping them dry on the back of her shorts as she hurried, barefoot, down the long hallway. She skidded to a stop in the living room, then tiptoed to the window. Standing with her back to the wall so no one from outside could see her, she lifted a tiny piece of the white lace curtain and peeked outside.

She took in a deep breath and let out a long sigh. She couldn't help it. The guy just made her giddy. Through a break in the thick foliage she could see all of the most important parts of him. Those parts that were at this very moment leaning over the folded car hood. He had taken off his sport coat. His faded blue jeans molded themselves around muscled thighs and hugged tightly rounded buttocks. Chance was by far the most delicious-looking owner of any car she had ever banged up. She had to clamp her lips down real hard on the overwhelming urge to smack her lips together and say "yum."

CHANCE TURNED AWAY from the Shelby, stuck his hands in the front pockets of his jeans and walked up the path to Hannah's home. The white house, with its Georgian pillars and wraparound veranda, reminded him of Mount Vernon. He had a soft spot for George Washington's home. Particularly the grassy hills behind the gardens. He had lost his virginity on one of those fresh green patches.

An old-fashioned brass school bell, green with either age or lack of polishing, stood to the right of the front door. He snapped the rope twice, the clapper clanged and mockingbirds flew from trees to escape the noise.

He didn't need his sixth sense to know Hannah watched him through the window. The curtain fluttered and he could see movement behind the lace. He jerked the rope again.

Fine, Hannah. Watch as long as you want. He had the patience of Job. He leaned back against the wooden door, folded his arms across his chest, shut his eyes and began to think of different ways he could torture Hannah for making him lose, even for a short time, the one part of him that had kept him alive. His hunches.

Only he must have been more fatigued than he had realized, because somehow visions of Hannah wearing a G-string bikini bottom and no top, lapping in waist-high water off the coast of Cancún superimposed itself on his brain, and it was Chance whispering to her, "Torture me, Hannah. Oh, torture me, please."

His shoulder muscles relaxed. Other parts of him hardened. He had just come up with the sixteenth way to entice the G-string off her when the front door swung open and he fell through, landing on the floor with a thud.

"Well, well, Chance McCoy." Hannah peered down at him, her smile sweet. Virtuous. "So nice of you to—drop in."

"Thanks." He leaned back on his elbows and didn't bother to hide the grimace. His gaze rose from her shoeless feet with their pale pink toenail polish, skimmed slowly past slender ankles, up rounded calves, great knees, perfectly shaped thighs, past a starched white apron that covered her from the top of her hips and over her breasts until he reached pale topaz eyes which caught and captured his stare.

He'd been right about one thing. Hannah, not he, did the torturing. Ignoring the wounds to his behind and pride, he bent one knee and patted the wood-plank floor next to him. "Have a seat, make yourself at home."

"I think that's supposed to be my line." She extended her arm. "Allow me."

Chance didn't need her help but he captured her hand, anyway, forcing himself not to labor too long on the way her slender fingers and soft skin felt against his palm.

He got up from the floor, landing close enough to breathe in her vanilla fragrance and see the light dusting of freckles across her nose and cheeks. He counted not one but six different shades of red highlighted in her hair and no dark roots. All the women he knew had dark roots. But not Hannah. Then, again, she hadn't yet done anything he had expected, so why should he be surprised? He let go of her hand and walked out of the house, stopping at the porch railing to fill his lungs with moist, humid air. Hannah closed the front door and followed him.

"Kind of hot out, isn't it?" she asked, her voice soft and lyrical.

"Yeah. Hot." Chance looked through the bushes and trees toward where his Mustang was parked. No matter what kind of sorceress's spell she had cast over him this morning, it wouldn't work. He was here to do a job. And nothing, and no one, would stand in the way. "Follow me," he ordered, jumping the three steps off her porch in one leap.

"Where are we going?" She hurried behind him. "Because I'm busy right now, and I was kind of hoping to just give you the key to the apartment, if you still insist on staying here, and let you bring your luggage in and—"

"I want you to see my car," Chance interrupted.

"Oooh, I don't really think that's necessary."

"You don't?" He stopped.

She missed running into him by half a toe. "Well, of course not. I've already seen it. It was a nice-looking car."

"Exactly my point. *Was.*"

"You're right. It was really nice in its day. Have you seen the new Mustangs? Very sleek. Smooth. Have you thought about buying a new one? Yours is such a wreck."

"The Shelby wasn't a wreck until you smashed it." He turned his back on her and marched down the walkway, breathing anger in, frustration out.

"Smashed it? I don't think so. I no more than tapped

the fender with the Tank. Isn't that cute?'' Hannah followed close on his heels. "I named my Volvo, Tank. I like Shelby better. Kind of nice. Is Shelby a boy car or a girl car?"

He reached the Mustang and spun around. She couldn't be for real. She had to be putting him on. No one made a fool out of Chance McCoy. At least not twice. His eyelids narrowed. "Shelby's not the car's name. It's the model. A 1965 Mustang Shelby. Very rare.'' Through a clenched jaw, he growled. "And you did more than tap it."

"You know, I really and truly felt bad about that. I said to myself after I backed into your little fender, and it was a little fender by the way, I could hardly see it...and I said, 'Hannah, you really shouldn't have done that. Why that car doesn't even belong to Texas.'"

"You said all that, did you?"

"Yes, I did. And then Officer Simmons came over and he said to me, 'Not another one, Hannah,' and I couldn't very well deny it. I mean the Tank's back end barely touched your front end, but it did touch it, just a little bit, not enough to make the car look like that." She pointed to where the front end of his car was having sex with the dashboard. "And it's my ninth, and I told him there was no need for him to worry—"

"Wait a minute." Chance held his palm in the air. "I must have misunderstood something here. Did you say your ninth? As in ninth accident?"

"Yes. That's right. And, well, you see, Officer Simmons has a bad heart and he doesn't like to do a lot of paperwork. Dyslexia you know, which is why he guards the parking lot. Not because of the dyslexia, but because of his heart. Nothing ever happens at the municipal building, not with my mother, the judges, councilmen, secretaries, well, just about everyone has a window and can look out into the parking lot and see what's going on—''

As Hannah grabbed some oxygen, Chance cut in, "Hannah—''

"So I told him I'd leave my card on your windshield and that I'd take care of the whole thing." He stared at the slightly sunburned tip of her small freckled nose. He took in her happy smile and her straight white teeth. She looked as if she expected to be rewarded. Or at least given a treat for good behavior. Well, she sure wouldn't get it from him. No way, no how. "You're telling me Officer Simmons let you go?" Chance snapped his fingers like Ada had done earlier. "Just like that?"

"Of course. Why wouldn't he?"

"Nine accidents, that's why."

"But I'm Hannah Hart." Her eyes widened. "Everyone knows I don't do these things on purpose. They just happen to me."

"How nice." Sarcasm dripped. "You're Hannah Hart, the mayor's daughter, and everyone knows you didn't do it on purpose, so you get off scot-free. Nine accidents, and no one does a damn thing about it. This," he spread his arms out expansively, "could only happen in America."

"I resent your implication." She raised the tip of her red nose aristocratically in the air. "It could happen anywhere."

He swore. Her nose stuck up even higher. Chance unlocked the trunk and lifted the lid, which still worked great since she hadn't damaged his rear—unless he wanted to count his fall through the doorway.

He reached inside, brought out a black athletic bag and threw it on the grass between the curb and sidewalk. Next he pulled out his suit bag and slammed down the trunk lid. "Forget it."

"Well, I really can't forget it. You brought it up, so it must be bothering you. And if it's bothering you and I forgot it, then it wouldn't be neighborly. And I always believed in the good-neighbor policy. So much so that I called my good friend, Ed Gilead, who happens to own the best body shop in town, and I know this from personal experience, and he'll be here to pick up your car this afternoon."

"Thanks. And while I really appreciate you going to all this trouble for me, there's still the little matter of paying for the damage. Did you call your insurance agent yet?"

"You know, Chance, that's a really good question. You're very logical. I can tell you're going to make a wonderful parks director. Logic is something most people don't have. Now, I'm very logical, so I can recognize that quality in you. But you just don't know the problems I have trying to get my clients to see logic. Why just the other day—"

"Hannah."

"What?" She looked at him, lips slightly parted, slightly moist. And she waited.

Oh, she was good, all right. Changing the subject, trying to throw him off track. Talking about clients? Logic? It wouldn't work. After all, she might be Hannah Hart, but he was still the one and only Chance McCoy. She may be charming, but since his body was already hardened to her charms, he could certainly get his mind to follow suit. "Insurance. The car."

"I'm getting to that."

"In this century?"

"You're in Texas now, Mr. Yankee. We don't rush things here." Hannah picked up the black bag, then dropped it back on the grass and walked away from him and his luggage. "Really," she called over her shoulder. "What have you got in that thing?"

With a drawn-out sigh of pent-up exasperation, he lifted the bag in his free hand and followed her up the path, around the big house and onto an old redbrick driveway. She held her head high, her back straight, and swayed her way toward the garage.

Amazing movement in her walk, he thought. Sure did explain a lot about the way she drove, since she didn't walk in a straight line, either.

Hannah climbed the staircase to the second-floor apartment and opened the door. He followed behind, enjoying the view. Well, a man *could* look. As long as he didn't touch while on the job.

Hannah turned on the window air-conditioning unit and dropped the key on the dinette table. "It'll take a couple of minutes before the room cools down."

He set the bags on the double bed and looked around. A small kitchen had been built along one wall divided from the rest of the room by a counter.

He gestured toward a dinette chair. "Sit down a minute, will you? I'd like to ask you something."

She sat. And crossed her legs. Then swung it, slowly, up and down, up and down. He watched and forgot what he had wanted to ask.

"May I say something?" Hannah's hands were folded quietly in her lap, in contrast to her foot, which was turning in rapid circles.

"Go ahead." He moved into the kitchen, away from her distracting legs, and tried to remember what his question had been. He glanced out the large window above the sink. The view overlooked the backyard of her house. Flowers had been planted in no apparent order, along pathways, fences and walls. Scattered, fragrant and pretty. Like Hannah.

Turning away from the view, which only reminded him of her, he opened one of the drawers under the counter, glanced at the silverware lined up inside, closed it, then opened the next one.

The moment he stopped looking at her, he realized that whatever effect she had had on him this morning was gone, because right now his hunches were bombarding him, telling him all he needed to know about Miss Hannah Hart and what she did with those Hunks she had boldly advertised on her pink business card.

He slammed the last drawer shut and turned back to the window. Dispersed images began to come together, to take form inside his brain until suddenly the big picture hit him like a bolt of lightning.

Hannah's Hunks. She ran a prostitution ring for women. She sold Hunk toys.

What a perfect racket for the mayor's daughter. Who would suspect her? Certainly not the police. Look at that Officer Simmons. The picture in his mind came in clearer. Innocent-looking Hannah, with freckles and copper-penny hair, made it a business to crash cars in parking lots. She looked for Janes, instead of Johns. Now that he figured out how she made her living, he'd do a little investigating on his own. Find out if the insurance agent, whom she didn't seem to want to call, was in on it, too.

She almost had a perfect crime going. Ingenious. Only she hadn't counted on Chance McCoy coming to town.

"I have to tell you I'm sorry," Hannah said softly.

He pierced her with his most daunting stare. She didn't flinch. Sure, she was sorry. She knew her whole operation was about to go down. Her Hunk toys would be history. Like the infamous LaGrange, Texas, chicken ranch. The one they made into that musical, *The Best Little Whore-house in Texas.*

"I know it's my fault. It's always my fault." Her head shook slowly from side to side, her hair swaying gently around her cheeks and shoulders. She sounded as if she couldn't quite believe it to be true. Hannah raised her hands, palm side up. "I'll pay, of course. You came here to help us out. You brought your car with you, and look what happened. It got all smashed up. Because of me." She hung her head. Her leg stopped swinging, her ankle stopped circling.

She looked innocent. She acted contrite. But he knew the truth. He retorted, "You're feeding me a line of crap."

Hannah rocketed off the chair, hands on her hips, all six shades of red hair a fireball around her face. "That's not so. I'm trying to be nice. But would you recognize nice? No, of course not. You're just a transferred Yankee, who wouldn't know the Texas style of niceness if it slapped you on the side of your head and screamed N-I-C-E."

"And you can spell."

"That does it." Hannah, face flushed, marched to the door, then twirled around. "And you can kiss my offer to pay for the damages to that piece of junk you've got parked in front of my house *adiós*."

"And speak a foreign language, too." He took five steps, which landed him directly in front of her.

"Now you've really blown it, mister." She poked her finger into his chest. "No matter how much my mother begs me, I'm not going to invite you to join me."

"Join you?" *The mayor was in on it, too?* No wonder she wanted the Texas Rangers to come to town. More Hunk-toy material to recruit. Chance clutched the tops of Hannah's arms, stilling her pointed finger in mid-poke. Her scent surrounded him. Her breasts heaved under the white bib of the apron. His mother had worn aprons, too. Hannah looked anything but motherly. "Join you for what?"

"The party."

"The Hunk party?" he asked sarcastically.

"What are you talking about?"

His hands dropped and she stepped back, pulling open the door, letting in the hot noon air. Chance took the wrinkled business card out of his back pocket, smoothing it. "Hannah's Hunks—We Cater to Your Every Need," he read. "You know exactly what I'm talking about. Hunks catering to the needs."

"Oh!" Her eyes lit up in recognition. "That kind of party. Yes. We do that all the time. But not just Hunks. I use all different types for the parties. Tarts are good, too. Everyone loves my tarts."

"You use tarts?"

"And madeleines. Have you ever had a madeleine?"

"Madeleines?"

"But ladyfingers are always the best. Still," she reflected pensively, "the Hunks are the most requested."

"Maybe your Hunks are what people in this Peyton Place town want now. And maybe you serve up tarts and Madeleines and ladies' fingers as your specialty du jour. But you won't be for long, when I get through with you, babe." He leaned against the open door, his arms crossed in front of him.

"Babe?" Her perfectly formed left eyebrow lifted. Her topaz eyes sparkled. "Peyton Place? Specialty du jour?" Then, she let out a long, soft whistle. "Oh, God. Am I slow. You know, I really have to apologize to you. I totally underestimated your thought process. I just thought you were a plain old parks director. Someone who played in dirt. Underneath that outdoorsy—" she ran her hand over his arm, lingering on the muscles above his elbow

"—mind of yours, is the thought process of a real amateur Dick Tracy. You're so smart. So manly. You figured the whole thing out."

Hannah passed him on the landing and put her foot on the top step. "Please," she beckoned him. "Come on with me. I've got to show you my place of operation." She went down three steps. "You're so quick. Intelligent. And a Yankee, to boot. I'm so impressed. Truly."

He put his sunglasses on and stood there, waiting. She had reached the bottom step, still pouring out enough sugary compliments to do her town's name proud, turned, gave him a saucy grin and crooked her finger. "Come on."

Chance hesitated. The distance between them, although no more than fifteen feet, was more than enough for his nerve endings to go on red alert. Something was wrong. Very wrong. He couldn't put his finger on exactly what, yet, but warnings were zinging through him, clamoring SOS.

Oh, hell. He followed her down the stairs, across the yard, through the back door of the white house and into a cavernous kitchen where the air was thick with the scent of rum and chocolate.

"Don't just stand there sniffing. Close the door and come on in. I want you to sample a little bit of what made me so famous around town," Hannah said. "My Hunks."

"I don't do hunks." How dare she insult his masculinity?

"Really?" Her voice caressed. "Not even my Hunks?"

"What do you take me for? Some kind of pervert?" He pulled off his sunglasses and glared at her, disgust churning in his gut. How could she mistake *him* for that type?

She didn't deny it. She floated past him on a cloud of vanilla, smiled her ethereal smile and docked her hip next to an antique wood table big enough to seat twenty, but only equipped with two chairs. On top of the scarred tabletop were eight cookie pans lined up side by side.

Inside the cookie pans, positioned in even rows, were small, semiround, squished-up brown balls. Hannah looked at them as if they had some magic power and swept her hand in the air over the top of the trays. "What do you think?"

Chance stared at her lips. Moist and pink and begging for attention. Then, he looked down at the brown things again. He knew exactly what he thought, but didn't think even Hannah would put something a dog left behind on a cookie tray and serve it up. That would be bad for the Hunk business. So he tried the diplomatic approach. "They look familiar."

"Do you know what they're called?"

"Yes. Yes, I do. Wait a second. The name's on the tip of my tongue."

"Oh, I know how those tip-of-the-tongue things work. Sometimes it's better to just let yourself throw out a lot of guesses and then see if the name just comes to you when you least expect it." Her voice sounded perky, her body seemed to vibrate under the apron. "And guessing can be so much fun."

He could think of more fun things to guess at than what was on a cookie tray. Like untying the bow of her apron and helping her take it off, then guessing what would come off next. But he was here on business, so those kinds of games would not take place. "I don't play guessing games."

"Not even one time? Even you can figure this one out."

He would have been insulted by the "even you" comment, except he wasn't so sure she was wrong. So he rattled off a list of possibilities, ranging from clay baseballs to abstract acorns.

Hannah's full lips formed a straight line, and for the first time since they had come into the kitchen, she didn't look at all happy. In fact, she looked pretty peeved. At him. "Look at them. Breathe in. Smell their delicious scent."

So he breathed in again, and almost got drunk on the scent of rum. "A solid brown alcoholic beverage made to look like a deflated basketball."

"You're not funny," she said testily. "These are Hannah's Hunks." She glared at him as if he were an imbecile.

"What!" He thought of Philly, for the second time in one day. And knew he was in deep, deep trouble.

"You thought my Hunks were something human and illegal didn't you? You thought madeleines were women and ladyfingers some kind of mechanical device used for pleasure. God, what kind of person do you take me for? I mean, do I look the type?"

He snapped his mouth shut. He wouldn't deny it. He wouldn't admit it.

"No one's ever mistaken me for running a house of hunks." She started to giggle. "Although I kind of like being thought of as that kind of woman." Giggles turned to soft laughter, which contradicted the stern tone of her voice when she added, "Only for a minute, though."

He ran his fingers through his hair. Maybe if he got a haircut, some air would get to his brain and he'd be able to think again. Forget the hair. He needed sleep. He had to recharge the old, worn-out batteries. Hannah. Lush, soft, enticing Hannah. He never wanted to see her again. He had to get out of here. His feet wouldn't move.

"They're famous, you know. Hannah's Hunks are the most requested item at every party I cater."

He looked at the brown things on the tray. "These?"

"Don't sound so shocked. Here." She picked one up and moved it in his direction.

He wasn't a wimp by anyone's standards, but he sure didn't want to put that in his mouth.

"Go ahead. You'll love it."

Maybe in his next life. "Right." He took what she offered, wished she was offering something a little more enticing, like herself, and chomped down. Chocolate, rum and sugar. And quite a kick. "Good." He dropped the rest in his mouth. "What's the alcohol content? Two hundred proof?"

"One hundred and how did you know? Can you actually feel the rum? Like they pack a punch?"

"You bet. Do you warn your clients to bring a designated driver, if they plan on eating these things?"

"You're mistaken. What you're tasting is only the lingering flavor of rum on the tongue. The effect of the alcohol is gone."

"I hate to be the one to burst your delusionary bubble, but rum is dripping off these babies." The second Hunk tasted better than the first. He took a third from the tray and held it out to her. "Here, taste one. Maybe you've forgotten."

"I don't eat sugar." She ran her hands up and down the sides of her hips. He followed the movement of her fingers.

"My neighbors taste test new recipes for me before I incorporate them in my menus. If the Hunks' alcohol level had been high, they would have told me."

"Not if they're too drunk to notice."

"The citizens of Sugar Land don't get drunk. Well, at least not intentionally. And definitely not on my Hunks."

"Whatever you say."

"Rum's only a flavor enhancer. All the potency has been beaten out of the batter during preparation."

Hannah watched Chance root around on the tray, as if there were one particular Hunk he wanted to snare. Poor man. If he was feeling any effect from her Hunks it was all in his head.

"Did my mother tell you anything at all about the party tomorrow night?"

"No." He grabbed a chair and sat down, pulling one of the Hunk trays closer.

"We're having a get-to-know-the-parks-director party in your honor. It was my suggestion and she didn't want to do it, since you'll only be here a short time. But I convinced her that the length of time you'd actually be in Sugar Land was of little consequence when it comes to having a party. After all, this is an election year and any reason a candidate has to invite the whole community to a party is reason enough to have one. Even if it's just for someone like you."

He looked up from the cookie tray. "Like me?"

"A Yankee."

"Thanks."

"No problem. No one knows you're a Yankee yet. And if you don't talk to anyone, just kind of smile and nod, no one will. You'll be fine."

He nodded and smiled and popped another Hunk into his mouth. He had a nice mouth. A firm kind of manly mouth. If, just for one time, she could feel his lips on hers, she'd die a happy woman.

Hannah took a plastic bag from the pantry and filled it with as many Hunks as would fit. She tied the bag off and held it out. "Here's your dinner."

He captured both the bag and tips of her fingers. "Thanks."

"You can ride over to the party with me, if you'd like."

"If I drive."

"Don't you trust me?"

"Of course, I do. You're a fine cook."

"But?"

"You don't drive like you cook."

"Well, then, Chance..." Hannah took back her hand and made sure she gifted him with her most charming smile. "I'll just have to work really hard to prove you wrong."

3

HANNAH WORKED HARD all right. At trying to kill him.

Chance knew it as sure as he knew the intense pain ripping through his mouth had been inflicted by her own murderous hands.

"What happened?" She ran over to where he sat, practically comatose, at the kitchen table.

He couldn't talk. He could barely think. All he knew was that he'd give Hannah the benefit of the doubt and assume she was crazy. Since the only other possible alternative was that she was perfectly sane and wanted him dead.

"What did I do?" she asked.

He glared at her.

"Why are you covering your mouth?"

Why? "Just give it a little taste." She pouted her lips and leaned over toward him, holding a tray of sugar cookies. She pushed it so close the aluminum edge grazed his chest as sweet steam wafted under his nose. The warm scent of sugar and vanilla floated around him, enticing him, pulling him in like a fly to a spider's web.

He had taken one. Why shouldn't he? Those alcoholic Hunks she had pawned off on him yesterday had tasted great. Or maybe he'd been too drunk, after the first ten, to notice what they really tasted like.

So he had taken a cookie and bit down. Deadly mistake. Chance massaged his jaw. The sharp pain was slowly ebbing to a wicked dull throb. He asked hoarsely, "Who hired you?"

"Don't be silly." She looked insulted. "I'm in business for myself."

Wonderful. A hit woman with freckles. Hannah placed the tray on the table and stood in front of him, her hands steepled at her waist, as if in prayer.

So the end came down to this. She already mourned his imminent demise.

Only he wasn't dead, yet. Chance leaned past Hannah and banged the cookie on the table. Not one crumb shook loose and the remaining cookies on the tray bounced. "Have you thought about marketing these as hockey pucks?"

"You know, that's a low blow. Really low." She glared at him as if he were at fault.

He dropped the cookie back on the tray. It landed with a clank. "Have you tasted one?"

She shook her head. "I told you yesterday, I don't eat sugar."

Chance tilted the chair against the wall, balancing on the two back legs and massaged his jaw. "You didn't say why."

"Why?" she echoed softly.

"It's not that hard a question."

"No. No, it's not." She captured her lower lip and gnawed.

"Well?"

"Well..." Her eyes widened and then she said, "I'll be right back. I have to go brush my teeth."

"What?" The chair dropped back on all fours as he watched her run out of the kitchen. His mouth hurt like hell, his tooth was broken, his ego damaged, and all he could think about was the way her bottom looked as she ran. He shook his head. He was a sick man.

Hannah locked the bathroom door behind her, placed her hot hands against the cold porcelain sink and took quick, rapid breaths. She couldn't believe she'd told him that. Brushing her teeth? Even she could've come up with something more original. She squeezed toothpaste onto the brush, anyway, then pointed it at her mirrored image. "Okay. Chance can't be another dumb, dead Dave."

Hannah stuck the toothbrush in her mouth and brushed slowly. Dave had come to Sugar Land via Montana and had opened a small sporting-goods store in the Sugar Land Mall. They had bonded almost instantly. He had political ambitions and she had connections. She wanted to learn how to golf, and he had the clubs.

They spent hours together on the golf course, at political fund-raisers, dinners and the movies, and their friendship soon turned to love. No one in town, least of all Hannah, was surprised when Dave proposed. After all, they had become Sugar Land's golden couple.

And no one was more surprised to learn that when Dave had left for Aspen on a business trip, he'd taken along his secretary, Gina. All cheaters do get caught in the end, and it was no different for Dave. He and Gina took a ski lift to get up some mountain and halfway there decided to do the wild thing in space. Only Dave slipped out of the lift and fell down through the thin Colorado air. Poor Dave. If he'd only landed an inch to the right, he would have missed that sharp rock.

The ski patrol found him, pants tangled around his ankles, private parts frozen in position for posterity, a smile on his face.

"I shouldn't judge all men by that cheating, lying, no good, dumb, dead Dave." Soapy bubbles formed at the sides of her mouth and green mint splatters hit the mirror. "Even if he told Gina he thought my diabetes made me flawed and he deserved the perfect woman. That perfect woman being Gina, the sex goddess with the postnasal drip. Men will do anything, say anything to get a girl to fall in love. I should know."

Hannah turned on the faucet, filling her palm with water. It had been a year since Dave had died. And until she met Chance, no other man had made her blood boil. What if she fell in love again, put her heart on the line...and was rejected? "Diabetes is part of me. I can't change it—and even if I could, I wouldn't. I'll tell Chance up front, and if he can't accept me for who I am—if it makes him think of me as less of a woman—then, I don't need to waste my time with someone like him." She poured the water in her mouth, swished it around and spat it back in the sink. She wiped her lips on the towel, straightened her clothes and headed back down the stairs.

Chance heard her coming and waited in anticipation. He watched her walk slowly toward him.

"Sorry it took so long," she said, coming closer.

Every muscle in his body tensed into ready alert. Hannah finally stood in front of him, her legs wedged between his knees. She leaned over until her eyes, nose and mouth were level with his own, and he still didn't take his gaze off her face, not even to blink.

She gently tugged his fingers away from his mouth. "Let me look."

No one brushed their teeth in the middle of a crisis, unless it was an excuse to do something more sinister. The minty fragrance on her breath could be used as a distraction to keep him from looking for the mickey she had hidden within the cleavage of her breasts.

Would she shove it into his mouth when he wasn't looking? If he passed out, she could have her way with him and he wouldn't be conscious enough to enjoy it. No way would he pass out.

He slipped his gaze down a fraction, to see if he could find anything. All he saw was pure heaven.

He looked back into her eyes. So innocent. So honest. Oh, hell, he was a goner.

"Please," she coaxed softly.

He decided to give in. If he had to die, at least his final view of the world would be the top of Hannah's breasts spilling over her apron. He would die in ecstasy.

He opened.

Hannah leaned further down, put her fingers on his lips, lifting the upper one a fraction. The tip of her moist pink tongue peeked out from the side of her lips as she peered into his mouth.

"Can I touch?" she asked.

He nodded. *Touch anywhere.* He was ready to go.

She placed the soft pad of her finger in his mouth and gently rubbed along the edge of his teeth. Back and forth. Slowly. He had been rubbed by many women. But no one had ever rubbed him there before.

"Hum."

"What does that mean?" His words muffled around her fingers.

"It means I feel something."

So did he. And that's what had him worried. When she came anywhere near him, he hardened. Not a good sign.

"Here—you feel it." She wrapped her fingers around one of his, then gave him a guided tour over his tooth. "Right here. Do you feel it, too?"

Boy, did he ever, and he wasn't talking teeth, either. He gripped her wrist and pulled her hand away. "Do you realize my mouth is at issue here?"

"Of course, I do. What else could there possibly be?" She straightened, looking concerned.

He crossed his legs, hiding the evidence of what her rubbing did to him. And all that bending over. Those moves had to be calculated to drive him insane, because no one could be that innocent. Not even her.

"What do I do with my mouth?" he asked gruffly, thinking about what he'd like to do with his mouth at this very moment.

"What a silly question. I mean, it's not a secret or anything. A mouth is a mouth. We all have them. Some people have bigger ones than others, I'm sure, but still—what?" She stopped, eyes wide, lips set in a perfect pout.

"You talk with yours. A lot."

"Chance McCoy, no one has ever accused me of talking too much. Why I'm one of the quietest, least talkative of all the people I know. I hardly ever say anything unless it's of the very most important nature. Ask anyone around here if I talk too much and they'll—"

"What about me? I used to talk with my mouth—now I sound like I'm eating marbles."

"That's not true, at all. Why, unless someone had heard you speak before, no one would be able to tell that's not your real accent."

"I'll be living on infant food for the rest of my life," he grumbled.

"Don't be silly. If you're so worried about it, I'll get my nail file and file that tooth down, and you'll never know the difference. You'll be as good as new in a matter of minutes. And then I'll make you a wonderful homemade breakfast. How would that be?"

"Are you kidding? Is that supposed to make me feel better?" He rubbed his gums, sure they had turned black-and-blue. Problem was, when he rubbed, it didn't feel as good as when she rubbed. He pulled his finger out, crossed his arms and glared at her.

"I offered to cook you breakfast and file your tooth. What more can I possibly do?"

He could think of several things off the top of his head, without too much trouble. After all, her lips looked soft and inviting, her breasts strained against the baby-doll apron she liked to wear and her scent reminded him of the sweet, warm cookies she had tried to kill him with—that did it.

Did she offer an apology for attempted murder?

Hell, no.

Did she try to explain?

Maybe. If you could call, "Oops, I must have forgotten to add water to those Butter Nuggets," an explanation for the rock-hard consistency of those little bombs she'd fed him.

Butter Nuggets? In place of butter. This, from a woman who owned a catering service. "Can I ask you a question?"

"Sure," she offered. "Ask me anything."

"I don't want you to take offense, okay?"

"Well, I don't know if I can say, 'Okay, I won't take offense,' because until I hear what it is you're going to ask me, I can't promise I won't be offended."

"I'm not asking you to promise."

"Isn't it the same thing?"

"Damn it, Hannah."

"You asked." She stepped away.

"Can't you just give me a simple yes or no? Why does everything with you have to be some long, drawn-out self-examination?"

"I'm—sure—I—don't—know—what—you—mean." Her words were clipped, a half beat between each syllable.

Chance had the sudden urge to pull her back. Then he wondered why he was acting like such an idiot, since she was nothing but a royal pain. Everywhere. He stood and moved toward the door. For a moment he thought he could actually see the brain waves working between Hannah's ears. Scary.

"Well, since you don't want breakfast and you don't want me to file the tooth for you, I'll tell you what I'll do."

Warning bells went off everywhere. His intuition started to overwhelm him with the force of a hurricane.

"I'll take you to my dentist and he can check you out. I have dental insurance, so I'll take care of everything," she offered magnanimously.

"Hannah, sorry to be the one to disillusion you, but dental insurance doesn't pay for the innocent party, like car insurance. Which reminds me, have you called your agent?"

"I'm so glad you brought that up." She took her purse off the counter. "Ed called about your old car—"

"Not old. A classic." Chance sucked in a deep, exasperated breath.

"So you've said." Her hand waved dismissively. "Anyway, he should be done in about three days. He's quick. And you'll be so happy with it. I know it'll come back to you in better shape than when you gave it to him."

"Considering I gave him nothing more than a twisted piece of metal..."

"You know what I mean. Ed has this way with cars. Makes them kind of purr. You may actually thank me for providing you the means to have Ed work on your car."

"Hannah."

"Yes?"

"The keys, please."

"For what?"

"Your car."

"I'll be happy to drive you. Really, Chance, you might get lost. Think of all the wasted time. I could give you directions, but I'm not good at that. I'll probably get you mixed up—"

"Or dead." He held out his open palm.

"Well, I never. In your weakened state, who would have thought you'd be so ungrateful?" Hannah hung the apron over the hook by the back door. "You may think you're tough, Mr. McCoy, but there's no way I'm going to let you go to my dentist without me."

"Suit yourself." A little glimmer of something akin to anticipation settled in the pit of his belly.

Hannah didn't bother to lock the back door as she followed Chance outside. The morning sun beat down on top of them. Even this early in March, the combination of heat and humidity seemed oppressive. The lightweight blue cotton shirt clung to her. She picked at the material, pulling it away from her skin, letting what little breeze there was whisper past, catch her, cool her. "I really am sorry about your tooth."

He grunted.

Well, fine, then. She had nothing more to say, either. When they reached the passenger side of the Tank, she turned to face him, leaning her back against the car.

"Excuse me." Chance reached around her, key extended.

Hannah didn't move. She supposed she could tell him the car door was unlocked, only he had these chocolate-brown eyes that left her momentarily tongue-tied. So she stared into them and tried to read the hidden thoughts in their depths. He could either want to pin her to the car and use her body as a dartboard or kiss her senseless. She'd guess the darts.

"I told you I'd pay for your tooth." Hannah broke the silence. "And the car," she added.

"I know."

"I told you I'd take care of all your problems."

He sent her a dubious look.

"I told you there isn't one single, little thing you have to worry about." She tried hard to sound convincing. She'd never had this much trouble making anyone understand her.

"Yes, you did."

"You don't believe me."

"I believe you."

"I can understand why you wouldn't." Hannah went on as if he hadn't spoken. "You hardly know me, at all. But I'm very well respected in town. I have a reputation in the community."

"That I can believe." His lips twitched.

"Well, I do."

"I agreed with you."

"You don't know anything about it. Everyone looks up to me. They hire me to plan and cater parties. I tutor their kids, I coach baseball. I do first aid. I know the Heimlich maneuver. People trust me."

"I'm not arguing with you."

"Yes, you are."

"Maybe. Let's go."

Hannah moved aside and he opened the door for her. She was pretty sure that when his forearm grazed her back it was an accident. Nothing more than a chance brushing of skin against skin. But the Indy 500 raging though her belly was anything but innocent. She glanced at his face, trying to find some hint he had felt it, too. Nothing. No reaction, at all. Now that would have to change.

She kicked a small pebble with her open-toed sandal. Hard. "Ouch."

He immediately focused on her feet. Just where she thought he'd be happiest looking. Sometimes men were so transparent.

"Does it hurt?" he asked.

"No." She wiggled her toes and smiled up at him, cupping her hand over her eyes, blocking out the sun. She almost felt sorry for him. Lines of fatigue bracketed his eyes, and she recognized the little sliver of shame running through her for what it was. Guilt for putting those lines on his rugged face in the first place.

She slid over the seat and slowly swung her legs around, gracefully, making sure the white shorts hiked up enough for him to see at least half her thighs. His thoughts, as far as she could tell, were off his tooth, since he didn't take his gaze off her legs.

"You can close the door now." She smoothed her hands down her shorts.

"Are you all in?"

"I'm in."

And still the door didn't close.

"I'm all in," she repeated.

He cleared his throat, then pushed the door shut. She looked straight ahead, and as much as she wanted to yell "Yes!" she kept her expression blank.

Chance folded himself behind the steering wheel and put the seat belt around him, snapping the buckle in place.

"I'll make you a promise, Chance McCoy," Hannah said softly. "I won't feed you any more sugar cookies."

"I'll hold you to it."

He smiled at her then. A real smile, this time. And that

brief upward twist of his strong lips gave her hope that anything that may happen between them in the future would not be jeopardized by a broken tooth.

He stuck the key into the ignition, then hesitated a moment.

"All you have to do is turn the key away from you," she said.

"Why don't you eat sugar?"

But would a future be jeopardized by diabetes? Hannah hadn't missed those flirting looks he sent her way, nor the hot hunger in his eyes. But would those looks turn from wanting to sympathy when he knew?

He's not dumb, dead Dave. He's not dumb, dead Dave. He won't think of me as less of a woman. An imperfect woman. He's not Dave. "I'm diabetic."

"Now *that* makes sense." Chance nodded, then turned the key and started the car. "Do you do anything to control it besides not eat sugar?"

"Insulin, three times a day. And I have to eat right after I take the shot." She studied his expression carefully for any sign he was put off. But the heat of his gaze had not cooled.

"I have to admit I'm relieved you're only diabetic and it's nothing personal against me," Chance said. "For a while I thought you were trying to kill me."

Kill him? Oh, heavens. She wanted to kiss him. To hug him. To give him as much happiness as he had just given her. A reason to hope and dream of romance once again. With him. And now that she knew there was hope, she'd make sure he also knew she was interested.

"Which way to the dentist?" he asked, backing out of the driveway.

She directed him west down Main Street and had him

turn right on Eldridge. "Okay, this is it. Right here." Hannah pointed left.

Chance slowed and turned the wheel right.

"Left. Left," Hannah yelled, throwing her arm in front of his face, knocking his nose. "Go left."

He twisted the wheel, tires skidded and the car turned in the direction she pointed. "You said right," he bit out.

"No, I didn't. I told you to turn, and I pointed. You weren't paying attention."

Chance clamped down on his lips and clutched the steering wheel tighter. "Now where?"

"Keep going. But go slow. I want to show you the park. Here, on the right." Things were not off to a good romantic start, that was for sure.

"I've already had a tour."

"I didn't know that. When?"

"Chief Turley picked me up this morning and showed me around."

"That was nice of him," she said, thinking all the while Chief Turley was a traitor to womankind, her in particular. "Oh-oh, here, turn right here." She slung her hand across his face again, hitting his nose. He had a great nose, with a lot of character. It had probably been broken a few times, so her hand smashing into it probably wouldn't do any damage.

Chance stomped on the brake and brought the Volvo to a screeching halt. "Which way? Right or left?" he ground out.

"I pointed to the left." She flung her arm left again. How was she supposed to get him in a romantic mood, if he kept acting stupid? "Right there is left."

"You said right."

"I didn't."

Stupid and argumentative, too. She could see now she'd

have her work cut out for her. Chance grunted something unintelligible, which she didn't ask him to repeat, and he turned the car left. As he approached the stoplight at Main Street, she said, "You turn right here."

He stopped the car. "We've been on this street before."

"I know."

"We're going in circles."

"I was trying to be a good neighbor and give you a tour. I didn't know the chief had taken you already. The light's green."

Chance stared straight ahead, white-knuckled fists clutching the steering wheel.

"The light's green." Hannah gave him another gentle hint.

He didn't move the car.

"Green means go." She tried again.

"Which way?"

He did not look happy, and she didn't think she had done anything to warrant being the object of his disdain. On a scale of one to ten, with ten being high, the romance so far between them was a zero. Bad news. "I had said right."

He turned.

"There's the sugar factory." She pointed to the tall red-brick-and-glass building. "We used to grow sugarcane in Sugar Land, but that was about a hundred years ago. Now we manufacture the sugar and grow subdivisions instead."

He approached the red light at Highway 6. "Don't say anything. Just point in the general direction and I'll do my best to figure it out."

Hannah pointed. "The medical center's up the road a bit. Can you see it all right?"

Chance grunted again, as he pulled into the parking lot, and found a space near the building. She opened the door, unwrapping her legs and lowering them, slowly, one at a time, onto the pavement.

Maybe, she thought, all was not lost in the romance department. He didn't take his eyes off her thighs.

"I READ YOUR X RAYS, and the good news is you won't need a crown," Dr. Topeck said through his blue surgical mask. "I can file that tooth down with no problem."

"I could have done that. I told him, too." Hannah peered over the dentist's shoulder and into Chance's mouth. "Didn't I? He wouldn't let me."

Chance wanted to answer Hannah with 110 reasons why he wouldn't let her and a sharp instrument anywhere near any part of his anatomy, only Topeck had two fingers and a steel mirror in his mouth.

"It's a good thing you fed him that cookie. Look at those cavities. One here." He tapped. "And here. Can you see, Hannah?"

"Um. Those are deep." She made a tsk-tsk sound and gave Chance a pitying look. "Your teeth are really white for someone who doesn't take care of himself. Must be in the gene pool."

He glared at her. When Dr. Topeck finally removed his fingers and the steel instrument, Chance said, "If I had cavities, I'd know it, Doc. I've felt no pain."

"You must have amazing tolerance, then. Because they're deep. I'm going to go ahead and fill them for you today. Once I start drilling, you'll feel it. What's your anesthetic of choice?"

"Give him sodium pentothal," Hannah said. "Then he'll have to tell the truth about what his car really looked like before I backed into it."

"You hit another one?" the dentist asked.

"Only a little tap."

Chance glared at her. "She killed it. Novocaine's fine."

"All right. Hannah, go tell Debbi Sue I'll be ready in a few minutes."

After she left, Dr. Topeck picked up the drill and turned on the loud buzzing motor. "Just testing."

Chance nodded. The message came through loud and clear and extremely sharp.

"You have any last words before we start?"

"Yes. Remind Hannah to use the ingredients a recipe calls for when she bakes."

The dentist laughed. "Poor Hannah. She's good at so much, no one has the heart to tell her the only thing she makes that are edible are those Hunks."

Chance heard affection in the dentist's voice. It was great that everyone liked her, but Ada could have warned him about her experiments. *Ha! That was a laugh.* Ada would be the last person who'd warn him. If anything, she'd purposely placed obstacles in his way. After all, Ada told him the apartment he was supposed to live in had burned down, but did he know that for a fact? No. Ada had insisted he move into Hannah's garage apartment. She had to know living near Hannah was hazardous to one's health. "Hannah may be good for many things, but she's an expert at getting into trouble."

"You're wrong, unless you mean that time with dumb, dead Dave. Grief can do that to a person. But everyone has a lapse or two. Even Hannah."

"Who?"

"I'm not one to spread gossip." Topeck pointed the drill at Chance. "You'll have to ask her about Dave yourself. What I'm saying is, even if you think she makes bad cookies, she did tutor my older boy, Robby, through calculus." The drill swung toward a family portrait hung on the wall behind the doctor. "That's him, third from the left."

"She does calculus?" Even Chance heard the shock, or maybe disbelief, in the tone of his voice.

Dr. Topeck acted personally affronted. "Are you questioning her genius?"

"Genius? At cooking? Driving? Directions? What exactly? Because I'm telling you, Doc, and I don't mean to be disagreeable, especially since you're holding that drill, but I've been with Hannah all morning and part of the day yesterday. She's far from a genius. She's a mess."

The dentist flipped his magnifying glasses down over his eyes and revved up the engine. "I've known Hannah since she was in diapers. Who do you think would be a better judge of her intellectual capabilities? You or me?"

The same sixth sense that had kept Chance alive two months earlier, when a crazed addict had waited for him on the other side of a brick wall with a loaded and primed semiautomatic, was now telling him Dr. Topeck was a very angry man.

Chance couldn't be wrong about Hannah. She was using him as a guinea pig, to see how much rotgut rum and how many cement sugar cookies she'd need to kill the poor slob who ended up married to her. Probably after taking out a million-dollar life-insurance policy on the unsuspecting fool.

He didn't appreciate Dr. Topeck's eyes being shielded by the plastic glasses, or his mouth and nose hidden under a mask. He wanted to read the doctor's face. But no matter what Topeck said, or how sharp that drill was, Chance had Hannah pegged.

"Debbi Sue," the doctor yelled.

"Is everything all right?" Hannah asked, as she followed the assistant into the room.

Dr. Topeck looked from Chance to Hannah. Then back to Chance. "Everything's fine, Hannah. And soon it'll be even better. Debbi Sue, get me the setup. The one with the 12-gauge needle."

Dr. Lopez looked from Chance to Hannah. Then back to Chance. "Everything's fine, Hannah. And she's in his own hands." Tom just gestured with his chin one with the syringe needle.

4

THE NOVOCAINE APPARENTLY hadn't affected Chance's lip movements, because when Hannah opened the front door that evening, his long, low whistle sent tingles spiraling up and down her spine.

And then, when his deep, sexy voice drawled—as good as any Yankee could be expected to drawl—a slow and lazy, "Whoa, baby," as his gaze traveled down the length of her body and back up again, she positively burned.

"I was going to ask if your mouth was feeling any better tonight, but I can hear it's working just fine."

A devilish gleam came into his eye. "I would tell you to feel for yourself, but if your fingers start rubbing my gums again, we'll never make it to the party tonight."

"Why, Chance McCoy, I believe you're flirting with me."

"Miss Hannah Hart, if I am it can't be helped. You look delicious tonight." He captured her hand, turned it over and kissed the palm. "Makes me want to taste. One small bite."

Hannah reveled in the unmasked hunger in his eyes. She knew, when she had decided to wear the oyster-pink St. John knit tonight, she had chosen her attire well. She was well aware of how the lightweight wool clung to her curves, accentuating the smallness of her waist and the flare of her hips. Under the knit she wore a Victorian rose-colored one-piece corset, made of silk and lace, with a built-in push-up bra. The undergarment propelled her breasts up and out, the soft, plump tops pressed over the décolletage of the bodice and scented in her favorite Shalimar perfume.

Hannah wore the dress with pride, her shoulders held back, her head high. She had no doubt she would be regarded by Sugar Land aristocracy as a woman with the utmost taste and discretion, no matter how low the neckline or how much the tops of her breasts were revealed to the eye. Because Hannah wore her great-grandmother Estelle Morris's 10 mm cultured pearls with the diamond-and-emerald clasp.

Four strands of lustrous beads draped her neck and breasts, each pearl flawless and perfect in size and shape. Each guaranteeing her the respectability and distinction of her background, her lineage and her class as nothing else ever could.

"Thank you, but there'll be plenty to eat at the party."

"We could stay here and have our own private party." His voice was low, suggestive. "Order Chinese for the main course and you can be the appetizer and dessert."

"Now, Mr. McCoy, I'm not that kind of woman."

"I know," he said contritely. "More's the pity."

Hannah was impressed. He was so suave. He knew all the right lines and how to deliver them. "Come with me to the kitchen," she said, wiggling her finger. She walked toward the back of the house, smoothing down the knit skirt, running her palms slowly over her hips, tugging away invisible wrinkles.

Chance followed several feet behind, whistling "Pretty Woman" under his breath. She peeked at him once from over her shoulder and saw his gaze riveted to her posterior, a satisfied grin on his lips. It had been a long, long time since a man had given her bottom that much attention.

She stopped in front of the kitchen table, where trays filled with an assortment of cookies, cakes and sweet breads were ready to be covered with foil and loaded into the Tank. Chance stood in the kitchen doorway, leaned his shoulder against the frame and crossed his long legs at the ankle.

"Love those socks." Hannah pointed to where a flash of red argyle showed beneath the cuff of his slacks. "Is that some kind of Yankee fashion statement, or does the color have more to do with your bullish personality?"

"Bullish? Me?" His tone registered disbelief. "I don't think so."

"All Yankees are bullish. As in stubborn and not liking spicy food."

He looked perplexed. "Are those related somehow?"

"Oh, yes. I ordered a pot roast in one of Boston's most exclusive restaurants. Bland. No personality. So I sent it back. I mean, I ask you, would you eat paste? The chef came out and insisted he had roasted a perfectly spiced piece of meat. He scoffed when I told him salt and black pepper were not my idea of spices. He was a tenth-generation Yankee, and I'm telling you, Chance, those taste buds are bred into all of you."

"Pepper's a spice."

"See? You Yanks are all the same. Pepper's nothing more than a bland flavor enhancer. You have to use it with other things like garlic and onions and hot Cajun spices. You'll have to come over one night and I'll show you how to make a real pot roast."

"You want to cook me a meal?"

"It's neighborly."

He ran a hand over his jaw, as if to remind her of the sugar-cookie incident. The look in his eyes went from laughter to seriousness in a matter of seconds. He pushed off the wall and moved near her. The two top buttons on his blue starched shirt were undone, the knot of the tie loose. Dark, springy hair curled at the opening, and she longed to touch it.

Hannah's palms moistened at the same time her mouth went dry. She moved to the other side of the table, away from his scorching gaze, as nonchalantly as she could in three-inch heels, taking the roll of aluminum foil with her. "So what did you do the rest of the day, after I dropped you off at the police station?" She tore off a sheet and covered a tray of brownies. "And why would you want to go there? It's not really a Sugar Land landmark."

"Chief Turley's an old friend of a friend and unlike someone whose name I won't mention, *he* knows how to drive."

"Did you see anything interesting? Meet anyone special?"

"Not really. In fact, he said you know everyone in town and that I should stick with you, if I wanted to meet people."

"What kind of people?" If they were female, he could forget it.

"Someone who can cook, drive, you know, your all-round normal sort of person."

She stopped covering the third tray and glared at him. "Why are you insulting me?"

"I'm not." Yes, he was, and they both knew it. He'd been acting strange since he had walked through the front door. And that was the problem right there—the front door. He should've come through the kitchen, as he'd always done. Only he had to play Romeo and come through the front, as if Hannah were a real date. And he knew damn well it wasn't, and he had no business even dreaming of Hannah in those terms.

What had he been thinking?

Hannah Hart was a distraction he didn't need, and as soon as the car-rental place opened on Monday, he'd be done with her. He could get on with his job and life as he knew it and not be at the whim of some woman dressed in pink, who had great legs and breasts that demanded attention.

So why was she looking at him through those long eyelashes, like she was doing right now, with hurt and anger mixed together?

"I didn't mean to insult you." He'd been trying to protect himself from nice women who thought of men in terms of marriage. Women like Hannah meant commitment. "I'm sorry if it came off that way. I'm thinking about you. Your feelings. You know I'm only going to be in town temporarily, and then I'm off to another job. And you can't deny the attraction between us. Only as much as I'd like to, I'm not going to act on it, because you're really a nice woman, and I'm a 'love 'em and leave 'em' kind of guy."

"Attraction?" she asked, casually, but her cheeks were turning the same shade of pink as her clothes.

"With you being single and me being single, we have to control those urges. We can't get involved. Period." For a moment Chance wasn't sure who he was trying to convince. Him or her. "I'm a loner. It's the nature of my business. You need to find yourself the type of guy a girl marries, has kids with. You cook." He shuddered, it was an involuntary reaction that happened when he used the words *cooking* and *Hannah* together in the same thought. "Kind of."

"I'm a good cook. I'll prove it to you."

"That's exactly what I'm talking about. I don't want you to prove anything to me. We can't be together, at all.

At least we can't once I get my rental car. You deserve more than a temporary affair with a stranger who comes through town. Even if that stranger is me.''

Hannah had a hard time keeping a straight face during Chance's blustering protestations to love. Only single men who thought their single days were numbered put up this much resistance. He had staked his claim on her, whether he realized it or not. He'd mentioned children, the marriage indicator. If only he'd mentioned a dog, too, she'd know it would be a sure thing.

She also knew, from all those Southern Lady Charm School classes she'd been forced to take back in high school, that the only way to get a man to realize how much he wanted a woman was to make that man believe he couldn't have that woman. Bring a thirsty dog to water. Take away the bowl. Watch them beg.

Hannah said, "I'm glad you brought this up, because I've got to tell you I've been thinking the same thing. You see I know that once you get to know me, you'll start thinking about me in a permanent way and I'm not interested in anything permanent right now. That's just the way it is with men and me. Once they get to know me, they can't keep away."

"Huh?"

"But you know, I was also thinking that maybe you're mixing up your own shyness with being attracted to me in some way. It's so hard. Moving to a new place, getting introduced to people, it's all very awkward. So you're latching on to me as a kind of lifeline, a security blanket. Only you're mistaking what you term as attraction as nothing more than friendship on my part."

His gaze traveled down her body, then back up. "I find it hard to believe that you don't feel some kind of spark."

"Well, you're good-looking and everything. And I'm

sure I have a spark in me somewhere, but not for you. You know, you're not going to believe this, but what I'm going to tell you is the absolute truth. I can relate to what you're going through because I went through the same thing. Once upon a time, now don't laugh, okay? I was a really shy person. And I had all kinds of crushes on lots of different men thinking that it was love, when in reality they were just nice guys, being nice to me. But it wasn't anything more than friendship.''

"Are you sure?"

"Oh, yes. It's true. Then I read *How to Be Positive in Negative Times* by Dr. Merfish Hochman, maybe you heard of him? He's very well respected in the area of acupuncture, and well—'' She opened her arms, palms up, fingers extended, letting him get a really good view of all of her. "Look at me now. I'm no longer shy."

Chance stated with certainty, "No one's ever accused me of being shy."

"Great. Then, you're going to love this party tonight. I can guarantee a Sugar Land party won't be like any you've ever been to before. But remember what we agreed. I won't be overly attentive to you, and you must make sure that your tongue isn't hanging out when I'm around."

"My tongue will be firmly attached in my mouth." He laid the sport coat on the corner of the table, and shoved his hands in the side pockets of his slacks, pulling the material taut over everything that proclaimed him man. "I'm ready, if you're ready."

Oh, was she ever ready. Any woman over the age of sixteen and under one hundred would be ready for him. She really had her work cut out for her, though, since he was fighting fate every step of his masculine way. He didn't have a chance.

Hannah twisted one of the strands of pearls between her

fingers in the area near her heart, drawing Chance's attention right where she wanted it, and waited, not saying anything. She didn't need to. The gentle clicking of pearl against pearl spoke volumes. "I'll need help getting the platters to the car."

He blinked and refocused back on her face. "Did you make all this food?" He massaged his mouth. "Or buy it?"

Hands went to hips, her chin jutted out. "Baked."

He grimaced.

She raised an eyebrow. "You had a bad experience, and I can assure you normally that doesn't happen. It's getting late. Freddy should have been here by now. I don't know what's keeping him. We made dozens of trips to the Monroe mansion this afternoon, setting up the tables, arranging the food, decorating, and could have used your help, but you were out playing with Police Chief Turley—"

"Who's Freddy?" Not that Chance really cared.

"And I resent you making faces at my hard work—"

"Who's Freddy?" *Why did she avoid the simple question?*

"And the town's intelligence for letting me plan this party in your honor in the first place..."

"Who's Freddy?" Chance didn't care who Freddy was, and he didn't know why he persisted in questioning her. He took a step closer and skimmed his fingertips up the side of her neck, stopping short of the sensitive pulse beneath her ear. *So soft. So lovely.*

She gasped, her eyes widened.

"Who's Freddy?" he asked again gently.

"My assistant." She had to get away from his probing fingers before she did something silly, like drop everything and use her own hands to explore his face and neck and his wide chest, and then, worse, check out his mouth with her own mouth, just to make sure his tongue was really firmly attached.

"I can be your assistant tonight." Chance's voice sounded deeper, huskier. "And I'm sure the food you made tastes great."

"All my pastries are demanded around town." She moved closer to him.

His lips had quirked into another one of those devilish grins he'd been flashing all over the place. But she would not be distracted by his smile, not this time. And to make sure that she wasn't, Hannah pivoted and went to the opposite side of the table, away from the electrical currents Chance's body zinged toward her. "Your help would be appreciated," she said.

He followed her. And so did the currents.

"I'm at your beck and call."

Oh, no, she thought. She was at his. But as long as he didn't know that, she'd have time to make him learn how two people couldn't control the whims of fate. When she faced him this time, her breasts skimmed his chest and her nipples hardened. She made an effort to ignore the effect he had on her, and to make sure he knew she was ignoring it. She glanced at her wristwatch, as if the heat of his body didn't make her blood boil.

"Oh, God," she groaned. "Freddy should have been here over an hour ago. Chance, I'm holding you to your promise. I'm beckoning and calling right now. We've got to get going. Can you lift that?" She pointed to a tray. "If you can manage it, please bring it to the Tank."

Chance glanced at the tray and scoffed, "I can lift ten of those at the same time."

"We'll see." The solid sterling trays had been passed on to her from her mother, and six generations of grandmothers before that. "It takes both Freddy and me to lift one."

"You've got yourself a puny helper." When Chance picked it up, Hannah smiled, noticing his slight stagger.

"He's not puny. If you don't mind waiting a few more minutes, I'm going to call his house, to make sure he's okay."

"Hannah, this thing weighs a little more than a piece of cake. Call later, and open the door for me."

He didn't falter under the weight he held, which Hannah thought amazing. She went ahead of him, stepping daintily down the stairs. He followed without a stagger. And when she opened the back gate of the Tank and he slid the tray inside, she stood close to him, listening. He wasn't even out of breath.

"Did you notice the trays still left on the table?"

"I notice everything." He raised his gaze slowly from her toes to her hair.

"Hannah—Hannah I'm here," Freddy Arceneaux shouted as he ran up the driveway, his large Houston Rockets T-shirt flapping behind him. "Sorry I'm late."

"Where have you been?"

"Mom made me baby-sit for Sarah." Freddy slowed down to an easy gait, eyeing Chance with a combination of interest and distrust.

"This is Mr. McCoy. Chance meet Freddy."

"Call me Fred, sir." He stuck out his hand.

"And I'm Chance." Chance grasped it and they shook. "Good grip, Fred."

"Thanks. So you're the guy who's moved in with Hannah," Freddy stated with a mixture of awe and disdain. "The whole neighborhood's talking." He turned to her. "Does your mother know?"

"He didn't move in with me. He's living over there."

She pointed to the apartment above the garage. "And it's a good thing he is, since he's been doing your job."

Fred's face turned a bright shade of red. "It wasn't my fault. I said I was sorry."

"I know, but there are two very important reasons for you to call me the next time you're going to be late. The first is that I depend on you to help me. And the second one is," she gentled her voice, "because I worry."

Freddy slid Chance a sidelong glance. "Well I'm worried about you, too."

Hannah put both hands on Freddy's shoulders and leaned down, looking him straight in the eye. "I appreciate your concern, my friend, but there's no need." She straightened and cleared her throat. "Let's go, men, and finish loading the car."

Three more trips and ten minutes later, the last tray had been stacked into the back of the Volvo. Hannah pulled Freddy's cap off and ruffled his hair. "I'm sorry you can't make it tonight. It should be fun. Chance, Fred's going to be thirteen tomorrow and I'm making him my special pumpkin-pie birthday cake."

"You're using a recipe this time, aren't you?" Freddy sounded hopeful. "You're not going to be making it up?"

"The recipe comes right off the back of the can, Mister Skeptic. What is it with everyone, lately? Of all people, I would have thought you'd have faith in me."

"Oh, Hannah." Freddy shuffled a dirty canvas shoe over loose pebbles in the driveway, kicking stones and dust on top of his other shoe. "It's just that, well, you know...I mean, remember the last time?"

"Freddy, that's not fair. You're giving Chance the wrong impression."

"No, he's not." He rubbed his jaw. "What happened, Fred?"

Hannah answered. "Nothing happened. Just a little mix-up in labeling baking chocolate. Just forget it. I have."

"Sorry I brought it up," Freddy said.

"That's okay. Come on, Chance. Let's go."

He winked at Freddy, man-to-man like, and opened the passenger side of the door for her. If she were a fighting kind of woman, she would have belted him.

"I'll see you tomorrow morning," she told her young assistant as she lowered herself into the passenger seat.

"I suppose you're going to give me directions again," Chance stated when he got in.

"Of course, unless you want me to drive. I already know how to get there."

"I shouldn't have a problem, if you get your signals straight. Don't say 'right here,' when you mean turn left. You're supposed to say right and mean right, or left and mean left."

"I know that. So what's your point?"

Chance clamped down on a retort, started the car and backed out of the driveway. He drove down Blossom Trail Drive exactly two house lengths, when she told him to pull into the third driveway. A white plaque, set back on the lawn, said Monroe Mansion—Historical Landmark.

"Why didn't you tell me we were only going down the street?"

"Life is full of surprises, isn't it?"

If she was purposely trying to drive him crazy, she had succeeded. Admirably.

Hannah opened the door without waiting for him and swung her legs out. "This whole street is part of the historical district of Sugar Land," she explained as Chance unlocked the back of the car. "My house had been in my family for over a hundred years. I moved in when I got engaged, since my mother got it in her head that it would be a nice house to raise a family in. It was too big for her, anyway, and she bought a smaller one near town.''

Engaged? As in engaged to be married? The ache he felt in his gut had to be from indigestion—not because he cared.

"Hannah." His voice sounded an octave higher than normal and he cleared his throat. "How come I didn't know you were getting married?"

"I'm not getting married."

"You just told me you were."

"I told you no such thing. Where do you Yankees get your silly ideas? Didn't I tell you back at the house, not thirty minutes ago, that I didn't want to get involved with anyone? God, it's a good thing I'm here tonight, so I can watch out for you. You need an interpreter."

"Listen to me." He clasped her wrist. So tiny. "You told me you were living in the house so that you and your fiancé could raise a family. Do you remember any of that?"

"Of course I do." Her pearls clicked together, her lush lashes blinked slowly. "But he's dead."

Chance watched a range of emotions flash across Hannah's face. Anger, hurt and then, finally, pride. His own rapidly beating heart slowed. "I'm sorry," he said and felt like a heel knowing that was a lie.

She raised her face toward the sky then looked back at him with a smile on her lips. "You shouldn't be. I'm certainly not."

5

CHANCE STOOD IN BETWEEN Mayor Hart and Chief Turley in the receiving line near the front door. His hand had been shaken firmly by older men, crushed by younger ones and demurely pulsated by every woman. And he hadn't felt one twinge in the hunch department.

He and Hannah had arrived at the mansion two hours before the party, to finish setting up. She'd had plenty of time to clue him in as to what was in store for him. She hadn't.

He'd always relied on his chameleon abilities. He could play the part of a tuxedoed Don Juan or a homeless bum in rags. During the past ten years, he'd done everything, been everywhere and seen it all. At least that's what he'd thought. Until now. Tonight, the women of Sugar Land had achieved, both singularly and as a group, something no drug dealer, no pimp, no white-collar-crime executive had ever been able to do. Shock the hell out of him.

They wore their bangs curled and teased and shaped to stand straight in the air at least two feet above their foreheads defying gravity. If he'd only owned stock in a hairspray company, he'd be a rich man.

Clothes were either shrink-wrapped to bodies or hanging like a tent over generous chests and hips. He spotted Hannah through the crowds, passing out desserts. She had one of the few normal-looking outfits on. That pink thing she wore was elegant. Those legs. Those breasts. He hadn't seen one person tonight who could compare with Hannah's natural flair for style and fashion.

He looked away from her distracting plate of baked goods and forced himself to concentrate on the receiving line. Everyone in Sugar Land had come to meet him, and they all liked to talk. When Hannah had said she was the quiet one, she might have been right.

Chance extended his hand to the young woman in front of him, glancing at her name tag. Corette Riley looked as if she was barely out of high school but wore a diamond crown with seven points, each point topped with a ruby. Behind her hovered Moose, her bodyguard. "Is that thing real?" Chance nodded toward her hair ornament.

"Mr. McCoy, this is not a *thing*." She gently touched the gold and jewels resting in the middle of her skyscraper bangs. "I'm the reigning Sugar Land Sugarcane Queen." She breathed through sinus-infected nostrils. Lifting her nose high in the air, she sniffed, "My tiara was designed by Tiffany's."

"Impressive."

"I know." The queen pivoted and haughtily made her way to the main hall. Moose honked and followed.

Two women stepped into her place.

"This is my daughter, Betty Jo. Shake hands with Mr. McCoy, Betty Jo." Mrs. Brunhilde puffed out her massive chest. Six chins shook coquettishly, as she pushed a younger version of herself in his direction. "Betty Jo makes the best fried-marzipan bars this side of the Brazos River."

Fried-marzipan bars? Did everyone in Sugar Land define edible food differently than the rest of the country? What ever happened to good old American pizza?

Mrs. Tinker followed, dragging her daughter, Tanya, by the arm. "Oh, Mr. McCoy, what muscles you have." The older woman placed Tanya's hand on Chance's arm. "Feel, Tanya. Oh, squeeze it, hon."

The last thing he wanted was for Tanya to be squeezing him anywhere.

"I bet you love to hunt, don't you, Mr. McCoy?" Tanya had a twang.

"I don't hunt." At least, not in the way she was thinking of. Tanya rubbed his arm up and down. Chance used every ounce of willpower not to jerk away.

"My little Tanya here is a great trapper." Mrs. Tinker looked him up and down, as if assessing his worth. "And she's been known to cook a fair meal, too. Now you come to the house Tuesday evenin' for dinner, ya' hear? She's plannin' on roastin' up that armadillo she caught by the side of the road last week."

"Why that's downright disgustin', Tanya Erleen." Merna Ferris shouldered her way in front of Chase. "Feedin' a man a road-kill armadillo, when there are so many more—" Merna scanned him "—delectable morsels to nibble on."

Durinda Daven's bony hip shoved Merna aside. "I'm a divorcée." She lowered her eyelids, giving him a good look at very long black false eyelashes held in place by thick, glossy eyeliner and a glob of white glue. "And available."

Durinda was pushed over, not so very gently, by Jayne Witherspoon's taloned claws. And so the Sugar Land bevy of beauties paraded before him.

Chance concentrated on each name and face. Any one of them could be operating a distribution center for heroin. Although he doubted it, since he hadn't felt one twinge. Every few minutes, a flash of Hannah would pass through his line of vision. She lifted her plate, filled with desserts, and mouthed, "Want some?" He wanted some all right. Just not what was on the plate.

The band's music vibrated through the floorboards, walls and ceiling. The chandelier's crystal lights bounced in exact rhythm. Hannah shouldered her way through the crowd until she stood in front of him, in between a woman dressed in lime green, named Spring Tyme, and a white-haired man, Judge Irwin Fine.

"Are you sure you don't want something to nibble on?" she asked.

"Do you cook armadillo?"

"Oh, you've met Tanya." She lifted the plate of pastries. "I was thinking about something sweeter."

He liked the way her neckline dipped low, revealing the tops of her full, creamy breasts. That looked pretty sweet. He could nibble there. The knit skirt outlined the shape of her thighs and just a hint of the heavenly juncture between her legs. A nibble or two in that direction would sure be delightful. And then a nibble farther up—ah, Hannah, he almost groaned, you may not be able to make cookies, but you sure know how to dress.

He took a Hunk off the plate. They were a known entity, but in case something had been added, like rock candy, Chance took a cautious bite. The Hunk melted on his tongue and tasted just as he remembered, heavy with chocolate, and oozing in one-hundred-proof rum. He threw in the rest, then took two more.

Judge Fine smiled at Hannah in a fatherly way and took three Hunks.

Spring said, "Oh, Hannah, I've been wanting to get me some of these." She daintily lifted several. The Hunks dwindled, while all the other pastries remained.

"It was good meeting you, McCoy." The judge

punched his shoulder while wagging his bushy eyebrows at Spring, who giggled.

Chance reached for Hannah's elbow when she started to walk away. "Where're you going?"

"I have a lot of people to serve."

To his right, Ada was in deep conversation with a string bean of a man holding the brim of a cowboy hat in his hand and the problems of the world on his face. On his left, Chief Turley made valiant efforts to disentangle his arm from Mrs. Muldane's vapid grasp. And in front of him was Hannah, who, by her very desirable position in the reception line, temporarily postponed the ongoing pageant of available women.

Chance leaned over close to her ear. "You set me up and you're going to pay."

"I did what?" Hannah swayed back, looking puzzled.

"The meat market. You owe me."

"I don't know what you're talking about."

"Yes you do. I'm the Friday-night prime-rib special."

"You flatter yourself, Mr. McCoy." Hannah shimmied her shoulders. "This is Saturday."

He looked out the door at the growing line weaving down the steps and toward the street. Young women and their mothers, preening into mirrors, puffing up already puffed-up hair. "Do you think those women care what day it is?"

"Did you notice them, too? It's really something, isn't it? Oh, I get it. You think they're here to see you." She laughed. "You're just a novelty. They came because of the band, Sweet Boots. Here, have another Hunk." She pushed the plate toward him.

"I don't want one."

"Okay. Try a lemon kiss. I made them last week. Guaranteed to make you pucker."

"I'll pass." The lemon kisses were blue. "I've never had complaints about my puckerer." He tossed two more Hunks in his mouth, anyway.

"I bet you haven't." Hannah made a soft, smacking sound, then disappeared into the crowd.

Chance watched her work the room. Women took cookies, waited until Hannah's back was turned, wrapped them in napkins and quickly stuffed them in their purses.

"Mayor." Chance tapped Ada's arm. When she glanced in his direction, he asked quietly, "Why are those people stealing food?"

"They do that all the time. Ignore it." Then, she ignored him.

Ada might think she could play the withholding-information-and-make-him-work-for-his-money game, but Chance knew he'd get the information he wanted. He always did. When the reception line finally dwindled down to a few stragglers, Chance told Turley he needed to talk to him. The chief nodded, then disappeared through the crowd. Chance again tapped Ada's arm. "I'm going to mingle."

She gave him a phony political smile and dismissed him with a wave of her hand.

"Before I leave Sugar Land, I'll prove to you that one Chance McCoy is worth twenty Texas Rangers."

"For the sake of my town, I hope you do. But for my own personal satisfaction—that being I'm never wrong—and for the advancement of my bank account, how about a wager?"

"You couldn't afford it." He'd come across too many people like the mayor. Skeptics. The only way to win them over was to win the war.

Chance scanned the room for a trace of Hannah, not even bothering to wonder anymore why he felt the need to find her. But there was a need inside him and it was great. She made him feel good. She made him laugh. She had an optimistic view of the world around her. Which couldn't be easy for her considering the everyday struggles she faced in her life. Not only was she a diabetic, she had Ada as a mother.

Chance finally spotted her handing out desserts near the band. Her insurance salesman, Elvin Evans, was sniffing behind her as if she were in heat.

He took a step away from the reception line when Ada spoke to him—the first time she had done so without being spoken to first. "My daughter's a trusting soul."

Chance didn't answer. He didn't know what to say.

"She's taken a liking to you, but she doesn't know what you're really doing here or that you're a dangerous man. As Hannah's mother, I don't want to see her heart get broken, and I know you have that capability. As the mayor, I hope you'll find the drug ring soon and leave town before my daughter falls in love with you."

"That's not likely to happen."

"Which part? Hannah's falling in love with you, her heart getting broken or you finding the drug ring?"

"I'll find the ring. The rest won't happen."

"And do you provide a guarantee, Mr. McCoy? A warranty, maybe?"

"You'll have to accept my word. Like I said before, you can't afford the bet and you couldn't afford a warranty, either."

"Do you really believe you have that much control over your life?"

"I've always controlled my destiny, Mayor." He walked away, refusing to admit the fear running through him—that for the first time in ten years, his destiny might be in someone else's hands.

Chance made an effort to reach the banquet room, but people sidetracked him, giving advice on how to run a park while Gus was gone. Not that he was averse to the guidance. His knowledge of parks was limited to knowing the difference between grass and asphalt. He knew he wouldn't be in the job long enough to make a difference.

Through the masses, he caught glimpses of Hannah offering a never-ending supply of desserts from the china plate she carried. The crowd seemed to love them, picking up two or three and placing them on a red, white or blue paper napkin.

When he finally reached her, she held the plate toward him. "Would you like some more?"

Chance recognized chocolate-chip cookies and her Hunks. Then there were little cakes, maybe brownies. And a variety of pastries defying description. "No, thanks." He patted his stomach. "Full."

Hannah nodded and smiled, the same smile she gave to everyone else, then continued on her way, swaying her plate and other parts of her from side to side calling out "Cookie, cake, treat. Cookie, cake, treat."

Chance stood alone in the middle of the crowd, watching Hannah head in the opposite direction. When had he started to think that her smile for him should be a little bigger, a little more intimate, a little bit more special than anyone else's?

He'd better snap out of it and stop acting like a sap. Think of the goal; finish this job before Jim found somewhere else to send him. Get to those beaches in Cancún, letting nothing and no one stand in his way. Especially not some babe with long legs, trim ankles and breasts that called out to him. Someone named Hannah Hart.

He headed in the opposite direction from the woman whom he was determined would have absolutely no influence on him. He shook hands, made small talk and motioned to Chief Turley to meet him in the room where the food tables and ice sculpture had been set up.

"You didn't see that," Turley said when he threw a handful of pastries in the trash.

"Didn't see what?"

"That's my boy. I knew you'd get along fine in this town. You've got to ignore Ada. She's got some powerful desire to get herself a Ranger."

"So that's what it's all about."

"Sure thing. You don't think it had to do with you personally? Nah. She has this thing about men on horseback."

"She made that clear from the first day."

"Ah, hell, that woman's been alone too long. Sugar Land is too clean a town. This drug ring is the first hint of a scandal we've ever had. So Ada, being Ada, thinks it's romantic to get the Texas Rangers in on it. Ignore her."

"Okay."

"We men have to stick together." The chief slapped Chance on the back. "'Course, if my ol' buddy, Jim, is wrong, and you don't catch those bastards, I'll have no choice but to call the Rangers."

"I understand."

They stood for a moment together, silent, looking over the crush of people. "Chief, I can't help but notice, and I don't need my sixth sense to see this, that I'm not the only one who has experienced Hannah's baking." People stuffed food in flowerpots, out windows for birds and squirrels, inside their sleeves. The citizens of Sugar Land had the disappearance of baked goods better choreographed than the New York City Ballet.

"You noticed that, son?"

"How can you not?"

"Do you think Hannah knows?"

Chance shook his head. "I don't think so."

"Good." A satisfied grin covered the chief's face.

"Can you tell me why someone doesn't tell her she can't bake?"

"Simple, my boy. No one wants to hurt Hannah's feelings. Now those Hunk things of hers are mighty tasty, and I'm sure she'll come along with the rest. Eventually. She has a good heart, and it's in the right place."

"Did it ever occur to you that if the town can keep a secret like the fact that Hannah can't bake, it could also be hiding the drug ring?"

"Absolutely not. Hannah's special. That sorry ass who's bringing a black mark on our town is not. Those scumball dealers are lucky it's only you who's here to catch them. If the citizens found them first, there'd be a lynching, and I can't say I'd do anything to stop it."

"I'll remember that."

They watched amid the loud music, shrills of laughter and boot-stomping dancing, as businessmen and -women moved to the corners of the rooms to wheel and deal. One person after another hugged Hannah, took her food, then disposed of it when her back was turned. "Chief, wouldn't it be a kindness to help her learn to cook?"

"You have to understand something. Hannah's been experimenting on recipes for people on special diets. Problem is, she thinks everyone should be on a special diet, and she keeps experimenting. Now, we know those recipes are going to work out someday. Until then, we're going to support her in whatever she does."

"But she can't cook."

"And maybe one day she'll realize she should have stuck it out in medical school. Or maybe she'll decide to go on and use that CPA thing she's got. But right now, if this is what she wants, then this is what we'll support her in.''

"She's a CPA? And went to medical school?'' The vision of Hannah operating on him seemed too real. She'd take out his liver when it was supposed to be his appendix, and then say, "Oops, no biggie, add onions, throw it in the food processor and we'll have pâté.'' Then she'd tell him to have a party, eat the liver and deduct it as a business expense.

He must have groaned out loud, because the chief was looking at him in sympathy. "Don't worry, son. Hannah's a genius. She'll figure it out.'' He smacked Chance on the back again and took off into the crowd.

Chance circled the perimeter of the room twice more, taking mental notes of the people who set his twinges going. Elvin did. But that could be because he wouldn't get off the heels of Hannah's feet. Other suspects were the football player with the crew cut, the man named Mac MacNaughton, who was running for mayor against Ada, and Moose, the bodyguard. But everyone was delegated to the background each time Hannah passed by. He took her arm. Firm and soft. She smiled, maybe a little brighter this time. "Couldn't let you go by without taking another of these.'' He lifted a Hunk from the plate. "They're great.''

"How about a brownie? They've been going over big tonight. Try one.''

"Why not?'' He took a bite. And chewed. And chewed. And chewed. Then tried to swallow. He looked around for a drink. Anything. No relief in sight.

"How was it?''

"Great,'' he croaked through dry crumbs. "Just great.''

"I know.'' She sighed, with a beauteous smile on her lovely face as she floated away in a cloud of pink.

Chance headed for the punch bowl, but before he took

three steps Judge Fine handed him a can of beer and winked. "You're not supposed to eat it."

The crowd danced and gossiped. Ada campaigned, and so did Mac. The chief kept making eye contact with Chance from across the room, pointing out different people and giving him the thumbs-down sign. Chance wandered from one group into another, making small talk. The focus of his attention always seemed to drift back to Hannah, as if she were the key to the mystery he had come to Sugar Land to solve.

When she passed him again, he captured her around the waist and pulled her close. "Let's dance."

"I have to serve."

"You've got at least ten helpers."

"You know, you're right."

Trombones blasted, drums beat loudly and the strings threw out a stream of vibrating sound. Dancing feet caused the wooden floor to shake. The singer belted out about some honky-tonk in Austin. Hannah handed her tray to the Sugarcane Queen.

Chance held her tighter. Lovely, soft breasts were cushioned against his chest, thighs on thighs, knees near knees, hips on hips, and all her womanly parts nestled just where they were meant to be. He covered her bottom with both his hands and moved her even closer, swaying in a slow two-step, knowing she could feel the effect she had on him.

"Ah, Chance?"

"Hum." Compliment time. She'd say, "Oh, you feel so good, let's get out of here."

"Are you tone-deaf?" she asked.

"Excuse me?" Was she oblivious to his straining body? "Are you tone-deaf?" Hannah repeated, looking over his shoulder, then to the side as people danced past them.

"Because if you notice, the band is playing something close to a jig, and people are hopping and bopping and you're leading me in a lullaby."

"Is this a proposition?" Hint—hint.

"Absolutely not! We already talked about relationships, remember?"

"You're the one who brought up lullabies." His hand delved into her soft red curls and he rested her flushed cheek next to his cooler one.

"You know what I mean."

"I'm a Yankee." He spoke loud enough to be heard above the music. "You have to spell everything out, remember?"

"M-E-N-A-C-E. That's a person who's driving forty-five on a sixty-five-mile-per-hour stretch of road. And all the people try to pass you by. Same can be applied to the dance floor."

To lend credibility to her analogy, someone bumped into Hannah's back, pushing her closer to him. Chance leaned her backward into a deep dip, using his forearm for support, then brought her flush with him again. "I'm a great dancer."

"You're okay, I suppose," she said doubtfully.

"I'm great."

The music grew louder, the beat faster. Chance slowed down even more, rocking Hannah from side to side, caught up in the softness and fragrance nestled against him. He felt as if he'd found a home at last.

And knew if he wanted to live, he'd have to find a way out.

6

CHANCE HAD GOTTEN UP at five, the morning after the dessert party, and fed the laptop computer the names of people who had stuck out in his mind. Then he sent the list to Jim through E-mail. If his boss had his computer turned on, he'd receive it within seconds and run the names through the D.C. database. Probably a waste of time, because the night before there hadn't been any strong twinges worth pursuing. Just a few false echoes.

He had already read through two years' worth of the Sugar Land weekly newspapers, the *Star* and *Mirror*. He had only made a small dent in the *Houston Chronicles* stacked along the side of one wall and had come up blank reading the police reports he had obtained yesterday morning.

When he heard heavy footsteps climbing the stairs to the apartment, then a loud knock on his door, he was relieved to have a distraction.

He shut down the computer and scrambled to the door, pulling it open just as Ed Gilead had his beefy arm raised ready to knock again.

"Car's ready. Let's go," the body-shop owner said.

Chance followed Ed down the stairs. "Hannah was right. You're quick. About three days ahead of schedule."

"Yeap. I'm the best in the business."

Seconds later, standing in front of his beloved Shelby, he wondered exactly what business Ed was in.

"Whatcha think?" Ed asked.

Chance thought he was being punished for the previous night. For dancing with Hannah, getting caught up in her softness, her scent, her warmth.

"Looks as good as new." Ed leveled an empty beer can with his lower lip and spat a wad of tobacco juice through the hole in the top. "If'n I do say so myself." He wiped his chin with the back of his paint-stained hand.

Across the street, Ed's assistant, Charlie, blew smoke rings through his nose, while waiting for his boss inside a purple '67 Chevy.

Chance circled the Mustang once, twice, then again. What surprised him was that he was surprised. After all, from the moment he had arrived in Sugar Land, nothing had been normal.

"You want to tell me why you did this?" Chance kept his tone soft, neutral. Deadly.

Ed shifted his wide girth from one foot to the other. "Well, you see, Hannah and me, well, she's my sweetheart. And no sweetheart of mine is gonna get in the back of any Yankee's Mustang."

Hannah, Ed's sweetheart? Did she know? Or was it delusionary thinking on Ed's part, just like the odds of Chance getting in the back seat of the Mustang with Hannah. The spare tire barely fit back there. And one thing Chance never claimed to be was a contortionist. "Hannah's your girl?"

"Well." Ed's feet shuffled. "She will be, once she knows how I feel."

"She doesn't know she's your girl, yet?"

"Nope."

"You did this to my car so Hannah and I couldn't get in the back seat of my Shelby. But she's not your girlfriend. Do I have that right?"

"For a Yank, you ain't too dumb."

"I'm not too happy, either." Chance's anger volcanoed.

Ed spat and wiped. "That so?"

"Yeah. That's so."

Ed smirked; sent a sidelong glance to Charlie before giving Chance his full attention again. "Whatcha gonna do 'bout it, Yank?"

Chance looked Ed straight in the eye, and made the one threat he knew would carry more weight than a fist in Ed's nose. "I'm going to tell Hannah on you."

"YOU DON'T LOOK HAPPY," Hannah said when Chance stormed into her kitchen. "Did you get some bad news?" She turned off the water faucet and slowly wiped her hands dry on the back of her shorts, as Chance advanced through the kitchen.

"Your friend Ed just brought back my car."

"That's wonderful. See, I told you he was quick. It's only Sunday, and we didn't expect the car until Tuesday. And you were worried. What did I tell you? No one's better than Ed."

"My Shelby's a red car." Chance took a step closer to her. "A bright, beautiful red." Another step. "Cherry red." Then another.

Hannah thought about staying in place until he reached her.

She liked the way her insides kind of melted together when he came into the room.

Then, again, she took a good look at the expression on Chance's face and decided now might not be a good time for her insides to have a nuclear meltdown. Hannah stepped back, then licked her lips and ran her fingers through her hair, but they got tangled. "That's wonderful.

Red's a great color. I like red." She held out a curl. "I guess I better like red. So what's the problem?"

"Green's the problem. He painted my car green."

"Oh. Is that all?" She sighed in relief. "Are you staying for Freddy's birthday cake?"

"Hannah." He took another menacing step toward her.

Hannah stepped back again and sniffed daintily. "Um, doesn't it smell wonderful in here? You're more than welcome to stay. I promise I didn't use Butter Nuggets."

"Did you hear what I said? Your friend painted my car green." Chance's voice deepened, his words clipped and precise.

"I heard." She wrapped the curl around her finger and wondered what exactly Chance's problem was. "Green's a lovely color. You know, I'll bet your insurance rates will go down. Don't they charge more for red cars? I'll call Elvin and ask him for you. Although I thought I read somewhere—"

"Hannah."

"About the correlation between the color of cars and insurance rates..."

"Puke green."

"What?" She stopped. "I don't think I've seen that shade. Can you elaborate?"

"It's the color of split-pea soup." Chance shuddered. "No one eats pea soup, much less paints a car that color. But," he laughed sarcastically, "did that stop your good buddy Ed? Hell, no."

"Okay, okay. I get it now. I've figured the whole thing out. Here's what the problem is." Hannah tried for the patient, calm approach. "You've never had good split-pea soup. I bet you've only had it out of a can. I'm right, aren't I? I can tell just by looking at your face." She beamed.

His lips were parted, his eyes scrunched, his eyebrows furrowed.

Hannah explained, "I happen to absolutely love split-pea soup. In fact, I make the best split-pea in all Sugar Land. Stay for dinner and I'll whip you up a pot. I'm all out of split peas, but if you don't mind barley or maybe navy bean—"

"You are totally missing the point. Again."

"No, I'm not. Once you've had good split-pea soup, you won't think your car's such a bad color. You'll be proud to ride around in it. It'll bring on warm, fuzzy memories of sharing split-pea soup in my kitchen. Of course, you'll have to kind of imagine the color green if we end up with navy bean, but you can do it. Just think of your car. Now, are you staying for cake or not? Because I have a lot to do, and Freddy will be here any second."

"You're coming with me." He grabbed her hand and pulled her toward the door. "To see what your friend Ed did."

Hannah tried not to think about how nice her hand felt in Chance's. But she couldn't help thinking about it, because his hand around hers did feel wonderful—and anything feeling that good had to be thought about. A lot. Only she'd have to think about their hands and fingers and knuckles and palms rubbing against each other another time, because she glimpsed the clock as they passed by on their way out the door and there wasn't time now. "I'm really, really busy." She tried to pull away from him. "My cake's almost done."

"Ed's waiting outside." He counter pulled.

"All right, you have five minutes. The cake comes out in six and I have to glaze it."

"All I need is three."

He held her hand all the way down the stairs and onto

the driveway. She wished he'd slow down a bit, because she wanted to savor each and every second of the five minutes their fingers were going to be connected. But he just kept pulling her closer to the street.

Hannah saw the car when they rounded the corner of the house. Her hand slipped out of Chance's and her walk had unconsciously slowed to a crawl. *Oh, God. Not even Ed could be so cruel.* Without looking at the men, she circled around the poor Mustang. The body work had been done to perfection. But Chance had been wrong about the color. Puke green was too nice a term. She tried to think of something uplifting to say. Something to make this horrible situation better. She tried to remember everything she had read in all her books on the power of positive thinking. And failed miserably.

Ed, three hundred pounds of muscle and fat, had fear in his eyes, sweat on his forehead and moist rings under the armpits of his white T-shirt. The dragon tattoo on his arm had deflated. He shuffled his feet like a kid who'd been caught with his hand in the cookie jar.

"Just tell me why?" Hannah wrapped her arms around her sides, protecting herself from further pain.

"Ah, Hannah." Ed spat into the beer can, not looking up from his shoes. A dirty white sock peeked through a hole in the canvas. "It's bad enough the Yank's livin' with you, but you know what they say about girls in the back seats of Mustangs?"

"He's not living with me. He lives over there." She pointed at the garage.

"Over there?" Ed squinted in the direction she pointed. "Well, that ain't the way I heard it."

"You heard wrong."

"What about the Yankee part? Have you forgotten about what that dead boyfriend of yours did?"

"Of course not. But Chance isn't Dave, and he's not a real Yankee, either. He lives in Virginia." Ed didn't need to know Chance had grown up in Chicago. Insignificant detail. Sort of.

"Okay, well maybe he's not a real Yank. But—" Ed leaned over so only she could hear his next words. "I'm not going to let some stranger come to town and drive you around in some hotshot pickupmobile."

"Pickupmobile," she practically choked on the words. She'd had a dream the previous night about Chance and her driving that bright red Mustang all the way down to Galveston and stopping at Make-out Point. Of course, she woke up when his stick shift got in the way of their passionate embrace. And just as well, too, since her alarm clock hadn't gone off. Again. And she was late for an appointment. Again.

Ed continued. "You know how many times this year you had to put the Tank of yours in the shop? And how many rides you needed? Well, I kinda like driving you around, Hannah, I just ain't gonna let him—" he pointed a split-pea-green-colored thumb in Chance's direction "—do it."

"Oh, Ed. You're so sweet, but you have nothing to worry about. Really." Hannah could worry enough for both of them.

Chance disagreed graphically.

"Hannah, can I talk to you?" Ed glared at Chance. "Alone." She nodded and they walked side by side across the street.

Ed looked down at her and said, "Maybe I shouldn't have done it. I guess I wasn't thinking too clear. All I knew was that if his car was in my shop, he couldn't be driving around with you sittin' next to him. It was a blind rage of jealousy that come over me, is all, Hannah. It happens that way to a man in love. And now you know my secret. How I feel about you. Men in love do things for no good reason. That's why it's called a blind rage, 'cause we're blind.''

"I had no idea you felt that way about me," she said softly.

"Well, I do. And I figured I better tell you, so you can let me know if you're worth goin' after, because I've got Betty Lou breathing down my neck to get hitched and, well, I love Betty Lou, too. Not like I love you. I've loved you since kindergarten. But, well, you know, Betty Lou is pretty nice, and I don't want you to get your feelings hurt or nothin', so I thought I'd give you first choice of me."

Hannah looked up into Ed's pale blue eyes. He really was an extremely nice man. "I'll always have a special feeling in my heart for you. You know that, don't you?"

He nodded.

"I've always loved you like the wonderful friend you are."

He nodded again.

"And I've seen you and Betty Lou together, and that woman loves you something fierce, in a different kind of way. Why she'd scratch my eyes out if I took you up on your offer."

He smiled. "Yup. Betty Lou is one spittin' wildcat, when she gets riled up."

"So you'll take back Chance's car and paint it right, okay?"

Ed nodded again. Hannah stood on tiptoe and gave him a kiss on the cheek. Together they walked back toward the pea-green Mustang. And toward Chance, who lounged against the Shelby, arms folded in front of him.

"I didn't mean no harm," Ed apologized. "Bad judgment on my part. I'll take the car back and paint it right. Have her back by Tuesday, as promised."

"All right."

"Do you still want it red, or would you rather I put it back to the original Wimbledon white with the blue rocker-panel stripes down the side? I could even add the Le Mans stripes over the hood, roof and trunk, at no extra charge, just to show you how sorry I am."

"You mean red's not the original color?" Hannah asked. "You've been making a big deal over this, and the car wasn't even supposed to be red?"

"The car's been red since I've had it and that's the color I want it." Chance stuck out his hand and the mechanic grabbed it, shaking hard. "Thanks for offering."

"Now that everyone's friends, I'll tell you what I'm going to do." Hannah smiled at Ed and Charlie. "I'm inviting all of you to come inside and have a piece of the pumpkin cake I made for Freddy's birthday. He'll be over any second."

Ed moved quickly toward the Mustang, practically knocking Chance down. "Wish I could, Hannah, but I've got to go get some paint, if I'm going to have the car ready by Tuesday."

"How about you, Charlie? Want to join us for some birthday cake?"

Charlie had the purple Chevy revving. "No can do, Hannah. Maybe another time. You don't know how bad I feel having to miss one of your cakes." He peeled out in a whiff of blue exhaust fumes. Ed followed close on his tail.

"I CAN'T BELIEVE this happened." Hannah blew her nose into the Big Bird birthday napkin and blinked back tears.

"It's okay, Hannah." Chance pushed his plate away and covered her hand with his own, squeezing gently. He didn't know what else to do. He wasn't used to offering sympathy.

"No, it's not okay." She took her hand back, reached for another napkin and dabbed her eyes.

Freddy gazed down at his piece of cake. His hand circled the empty glass of milk and a white mustache covered the peach fuzz on his upper lip.

The birthday pumpkin cake, minus three slices, sat on a crystal plate in the middle of the table. Thirteen candles, wicks burned, were still half-buried.

"First Ed brings back a green car, and now this." Her voice was husky with unshed tears. "Is this the worst birthday you ever had, Freddy?"

"Naw. Last year was." He faced Chance. "My sister gave me her chicken pox. I told her I wanted a puppy."

"I remember." Hannah patted Freddy's hand. "But didn't it turn out to be the best birthday you ever had?"

Chance could feel the enthusiasm pouring from Freddy's body. How long had it been since he'd seen youth look that innocent, that joyful? Too long.

"Hannah knows everyone," Freddy boasted. "So she calls up her friend at NASA and tells him about me and my chicken pox, and he said he'd take care of it. Next thing you know I get this phone call, and it's the astronauts on the shuttle *Atlantis*. Calling from way up in space. And they sang 'Happy Birthday.' I couldn't believe it."

Freddy looked at Hannah as if she were the Greatest American Hero. She patted his hand, then turned to Chance. "Tell us about your best birthday."

Chance leaned back in the upholstered chair he had brought into the kitchen from the dining room. It was easy for him to get caught up in Hannah's enthusiasm. "My sixteenth," he told them. "That's when my dad gave me the Shelby."

"No wonder you love that old car so much."

"Classic."

"Classic." With her elbow on the table and her chin resting in the palm of her hand, she stared at him through golden eyes. "Do you see your parents a lot?"

"My dad died a couple of months after he gave me the car. Then my sister, Nina, went off the deep end, got caught up in drugs and died two years later of a heroin overdose."

Hannah's eyes widened. She reached out and captured his hand, squeezing gently. "I'm so sorry. I didn't know."

"I am what I am today because of Nina." Only Jim knew the reason behind Chance's avenging pursuit of anyone who put heroin on the streets. His success rate had as much to do with Nina's death as his sixth sense.

He wanted Hannah to know about Nina. He knew he'd find the Sugar Land ring and he'd find them soon. When she found out the real reason he had come to town, she'd understand why he'd have to leave again.

Chance pulled his hand out from hers, narrowed his eyes and shook a finger at Freddy. "Drugs kill. Keep away from them, no matter what your friends say. Understand?"

"Yes, sir."

"Is your mother alive?" Hannah asked.

"Alive and well and living in Chicago. And she's a great cook. Taught me everything I know." He could smile again.

Tears filled the corners of Hannah's eyes. She said shakily, "I'm a terrible, terrible person to be with on birthdays. First, I destroy the wonderful car your father gave you. Then, Freddy's birthday cake. I've never cooked anything that tasted this awful."

"That's not exactly true," Chance started. "Your cooking the other night—"

Freddy shook his head wildly at Chance, his expression panicky. Chance decided to heed the boy's warning. For now.

"What about the other night?" Hannah looked from one to the other.

"Nothing. Everything's wonderful."

Someone would have to tell her, though. And soon, because the farce the whole town was putting on was ridiculous. In the end, when she found out—and she would find out—the truth would only hurt her more.

"Those sugar cookies were an accident. I was experimenting with Butter Nuggets. When are you going to believe me?"

"I believe you." Chance gathered the paper plates and tossed them in the trash can.

Hannah picked up the cake knife, and with the flat side, pushed down on top of the remaining cake. The texture was moist and springy. A sham. Its color was a light ivory-orange, just like the picture on the back of the can. The spicy, sweet scent of cinnamon and tangy fragrance of cloves permeated the kitchen, surrounding them with warmth, yet mocking them at the same time.

"I don't get it," Hannah sighed. "I can read instructions. I can follow directions. I'll admit, I try to be creative, and sometimes those efforts fail, like those sugar cookies."

She dropped the knife on the table. "But more times than not, I'm very successful. Just look at the brownies I served last night. Everyone raved about them, and I had switched from using sweet chocolate to sugar-free chocolate syrup."

"I ate a brownie." Chance took a gulp of milk. The thought made him crave liquids. He stuck a finger into the pumpkin-cake glaze and licked it, then went for more. "This frosting's great."

"Well, I had the powdered sugar, butter and vanilla. And, of course, water. I always have lots of water."

"When you say you had those ingredients, are you implying some were missing?"

"Maybe, in so many words, you could interpret it to mean that. Nothing that should have made any difference, though. I used substitutions. But it should have worked out fine."

"Why don't you give me a 'for instance'?" he asked.

"Well, okay. I guess I ran out of flour."

"What do you mean, you guess? Either you did or you didn't."

"All right. I ran out. My assistant, over there, was supposed to put it on the list."

"I did," Freddy said. "I don't know why. You never look at the lists I make, anyway."

"I do, too. I look at them all the time. It's just that I forget, sometimes, to bring them with me to the grocery store. I try and use my memory. It's important to use your brain cells, otherwise they die and never come back."

"Hannah." The one thing Chance had learned about her was that when she got rolling, it could be an hour before she made a full circle back to where the conversation had left off. "So you made this cake without flour."

"I used pancake mix. Pancake mix is good." She nodded in agreement with herself. "It does the same thing."

"How do you figure?" Chance tried not to grimace.

"You use flour to make pancakes, right? So why not use pancake mix to make cake?"

"Why not? Makes sense to me. I don't know why it does, but it does."

"And then there was the sugar."

"You said you had sugar."

"I have plenty of sugar."

"What's the problem, then?"

"I can't eat sugar, and I wanted to share in Freddy's cake, and so I replaced sugar with artificial sweetener. Half granulated, like regular sugar, half liquid. In case one worked better than the other, they would even themselves out."

"Are you serious?"

"I don't joke about my baking," she said self-righteously. "The recipe called for a teaspoon of salt, but I didn't want to put in too much because, frankly, Chance, salt's not healthy. And I've been a little stressed lately."

"You've been stressed? What about me? What about my car, then my tooth, then my apartment burning down, which put me over there?" He pointed in the direction of the garage. "In that bed that's not long enough for me to spread out in."

She swallowed hard, looking down the length of him. "Chance. Your voice is rising. I knew I should have left out the salt completely. If I had known you'd be sharing the cake, and that you have high blood pressure, I would never have even put in the pinch I did."

"I don't have high blood pressure," he said, seething.

"It's a good thing I ran out of vegetable oil, too. If you have high blood pressure and are under a lot of stress at least olive oil has the good cholesterol in it."

Freddy shuddered. "Ah, Hannah, that's disgusting."

"Did you think you were making a Caesar salad?" Chance bellowed.

"I'm ignoring that comment." She straightened her shoulders and lifted up her chin.

It was a move Chance had learned to recognize as an indication that Hannah was switching to fighting mode.

"I added the eggs, one at a time, just like the recipe called for. I only had two eggs, not three. And I only used the egg whites, not the yokes, because of the cholesterol and fat content and everything. So I added some water, to make up for the missing egg, and then used yellow food coloring to make it look like a yoke.'' She took a breath. ''What's the matter?''

''Nothing.''

''Your mouth is hanging open.''

He snapped it shut.

''That's better. Then, I added a little bit more pumpkin, because I didn't want to throw all that extra pumpkin away.''

His mouth opened and closed again, only he couldn't push the words out.

''Chance? Are you okay? Are you listening to me?''

''I'm listening. I'm not sure I heard right.''

''You know what?'' Hannah smacked the palm of her hand against her forehead. ''I can't believe I didn't realize this before, but I finally figured out what went wrong.'' She took a deep, cleansing breath. ''Yes, this has to be the problem. Everything's falling into place now.''

''You know where you went wrong?''

''I ran out of baking powder, so I used baking soda. That has to be why the cake tastes like cardboard. Because everything else I used shouldn't have caused it to come out this way. So by process of elimination, I've figured out the problem. And believe me when I tell you I won't make that mistake again.''

''Hannah, I hate to be the one to break the news to you, but the whole cake is a mistake. You made a pumpkin cake and the only ingredient you used from the recipe was pumpkin.''

''I told you, I substituted. Everything theoretically should have been perfect.''

"That does it." He threw up his arms. "You're a lost cause."

"I have no idea what you're talking about." She raised her chin even higher in the air.

"We need to have a talk." He'd bring her back down to the blue-collar level in no time at all.

"Oh, oh." Freddy bolted up from the chair. "Thanks Hannah. I loved my cake. It's the thought that counts. You're terrific. Really. And thanks for the Astros T-shirt. It's great. Gotta go." Freddy rushed out the back door, slamming it behind him.

"He was certainly in a hurry. He must have a new girl-friend. Isn't young love wonderful?" She sighed.

"Yeah, great. Listen, Hannah, there's something **you** should know," Chance started to say. He had to tell her about her cooking, because he couldn't become part of the lie. Although he almost laughed at himself over that sudden pang of morality. The life he led every day was nothing but a lie.

But then he looked into her eyes, the lashes still moist and clinging together. Her skin was pale and her nose was still red from sniffing back tears. And he couldn't do it. At least not today. He looked down at his hands, then over to her legs. Her legs were so long, he thought, and that's when he noticed the almost transparent half-moon-shaped birthmark on her knee. If she hadn't had her legs crossed, and the light hadn't been just so, he probably would never have seen it. But there it was, a crescent moon. Smiling at him. And there was a little freckle right above it. Almost like a wink. Daring him to tell her what everyone in Sugar Land had kept secret.

If he told her now, he'd never get anyone in town to confide in him. If he didn't become part of their conspiracy, he would be betraying their unspoken trust.

"What do you want to talk about? As if I can't already guess."

"Tell me what you think."

"You don't like my creativity. You think I shouldn't experiment."

"I don't know if I'd go as far as that."

"Good. Because with my diabetes, it's really important for me to create recipes for people on restricted diets. I didn't mean to do that with Freddy's cake, but the sugar cookies were a good example. Replacing the butter with Butter Nuggets. It didn't turn out, but you win some, you lose some."

Chance leaned over, elbows on his knees, both hands cupping his chin, as he stared into her topaz eyes. "I wasn't kidding when I told you my mother taught me how to cook."

"I didn't think you were." She smiled at him, and then snagged her fingers through her hair.

"I'd like nothing more than to give you a cooking lesson or two."

"Well, I suppose I could let you give me a few pointers, but you'll have to let me do you a favor in return."

"Sounds fair. What do you suggest?" *Back massage would be good.*

"I'm going to let you help me coach my baseball team."

"That's doing me a favor?"

"It's great exercise."

Not what he had expected, but it had possibilities. Watching her bending over home plate, chasing her around bases. A female baseball team. He liked the idea. "Okay." He wouldn't even mention the fact that he didn't know a thing about coaching—or baseball. "I can do this. It's in my job description as parks director."

"Well, you're technically right, but Elvin's job as head of the league is to get the coaches together, make sure the food for the concession stand is ordered and deposit the money into the bank. There was a big fight about it last year, and it ended up being fought out before city council."

"Elvin? The guy who was dogging your footsteps last night?"

"Did you notice that? Don't be too hard on him. He's divorced, you know."

Chance grunted.

"I'm the team manager and Freddy's my assistant, but I need a head coach and you'd be just right." Hannah smiled a smile as bright as a full noontime sun. "This is perfect. Just absolutely the most perfect solution in the whole world."

She left her chair and stood over him. Then she bent down, put both her arms around his neck, lowered her head and gave him a kiss full on the lips. It was only a brief kiss, just a friendly kind of thank-you kiss. Only somehow, his toes curled and his body heated and his lips, where her lips had touched, burned.

"Tomorrow, I'll take you to pick up your rental car. Would you like to go to a movie tonight?"

He said yes before he could stop the word from coming out of his mouth. And he hoped he wouldn't regret it. He could make all the excuses in the world about why he wanted to spend time with her. But when it came right down to it, there was only one. He didn't want to make the crescent moon frown.

7

CHANCE SHOULD HAVE KNOWN before they left for the movie theater that being a passenger in an automobile with Hannah behind the wheel would be no different than wearing red in front of a raging bull. Potentially fatal.

Very slowly, very carefully, he picked his head up off the dashboard after she brought the Tank to a screeching stop in the Majestic's parking lot.

"We made it just in time." Hannah sounded jubilant. She cut the engine, dropped the keys into her purse and pulled out a tube of lipstick.

He cautiously shifted his torso in her direction, taking great care not to make scrambled eggs out of his already shaken brains. Barely containing his anger, he ground out, "We have to talk."

"Sure, I'd love to later. But the movie starts in exactly seventeen minutes, and we can't be late." She looked into the rearview mirror and quickly reapplied pink color to her lips.

How could she do that? Get on with her life as if the past twenty minutes hadn't happened. As if they hadn't almost died at least three times. "Not later. Now."

She blended the lipstick with her pinkie, then dropped the tube in her purse and patted his knee. "Later. Try and understand. I'm on a very restricted diet, so whereas someone like you can eat anything, I can't. One of the few food pleasures I have is the Majestic's hot, real butter, buttered popcorn. They pop it at exactly fifteen minutes before the hour. Every hour. When it first comes out of the popper, the butter actually sizzles. It's practically orgasmic." She reached for the door handle. "I'd love to talk to you now, but I have priorities."

"Do you realize what you've done?"

"Put on lipstick?" she asked wide-eyed.

"Your driving." He kept his voice controlled, his anger in check. "You almost got us killed."

"Stop yelling."

"I'm not yelling."

"You may not be *yelling* yelling, but the tone of your voice is a yell, all the same. It's getting a little old, the way you criticize me. My cooking. My driving. Not being able to tell when a yell is a yell, even if it's not a yell. What's next? The way I dress?" She paused a moment, lowered her voice to almost a whisper. "The way I kiss?"

Kiss? Never the way she kissed. He had only tasted her soft lips for a brief moment that afternoon, but that was more than enough to make him crave more. "A lot of good kissing you is going to do me, if I'm dead. You have some desire to put an end to my life, don't you? That's why you drove in front of the freight train as it came barreling down the tracks, on my side of the car."

"That's silly. The train was a good twenty feet away."

"There wasn't even time for my life to flash before my eyes."

"Oh, please. Aren't you being a little melodramatic?"

Melodramatic? Him—Chance McCoy? No way in hell.

Hannah earnestly explained, "If you were going to die, your life would have flashed before your eyes. Everyone knows that." She glanced at her watch, pursed her lips and spoke faster. "When you're in danger, although, person-ally, I don't see how a parks-and-recreation director could

ever be in any danger except if a tree was to fall on top
of you. But that's not likely to happen, since you're not a
forest ranger. Anyway, if you don't see your life flash before your eyes, then you're going to live. If you do see
your life flash before your eyes, then you're going to die.
And by that time, it's already too late to do anything about
it. So, why don't you lighten up a little. Do you feel better
now? Good. Let's go.''

"A freight train was coming at us," he repeated through
clenched teeth.

"How was I supposed to know they finally had those
railroad crossings fixed? Am I psychic? Those arms had
been down for the last two weeks. Okay, let's go.''

"Hannah—''

She rolled her eyes. "And before you bring it up, I'll
tell you why I ran the stop sign. You make me nervous.
It's all your fault. Now, get out of the car. Time's wasting.''

"I make you nervous?" He laughed sarcastically.
"What kind of state is this that gives someone like you a
driver's license?''

"Thanks, okay, Chance. Us real Texans understand your
problem. We're used to people like you blaming Texas
when you can't cut it here in the real world, where men
are men and women are women and you Yanks are nothing
but coffeehouse cowboys. Now, get out of my car." She
pushed his shoulder. He didn't budge. "Okay, be a slug.
Sit here. I'm going in.''

"I'll show you a slug, Miss Drive-Like-a-Tart Hart.''
Chance stormed out of the car and over to the driver's
side, yanking open the door and pulling her to him. He
leaned her back against the metal, her breasts pillowing
his chest, her stomach against his waist, her lips touching

his jaw, her womanly softness cradling those hard parts that made him a man.

His gaze skimmed across pale golden eyes, thick black lashes, the splay of freckles across the top of her cheeks and upturned nose. The tip of her tongue left a moist trail across her full, sweet lips. His eyelids lowered, blocking out the afternoon sun, leaving only images of Hannah, her scent, her softness. He lowered his mouth closer to hers until it barely hovered above, separated by no more than a wisp of air.

She drew in a quick breath and touched him with her tongue. That one moist touch undid him. He captured her with an intensity he had been suppressing since their first kiss. Since the first time he had seen her in the mayor's office. He cupped the side of her face, buried his fingers into her mass of auburn curls, his thumb rubbing the sensitive skin beneath her ear. He teased her lips, his tongue outlining their shape, until she sighed and opened for him, allowing him to stroke and feast.

She wrapped her arms around his shoulders, her fingers kneading the back of his neck, working magic, sending electric surges through him. She pressed her body more intimately nearer to his.

When he heard the soft moan pour from her throat, he broke their kiss and stepped back from her heat, her embrace, her magic, and stared, taking in the dewy look in her eyes, the soft smile, the pink blush staining her cheeks. She touched her kiss-swollen lips, the lips he had branded.

He realized, then, that life as he had known it had taken a detour and he didn't have a road map to find his way back. He had become distracted by her and had to fight himself to gain control. To remember the reason he had come to Sugar Land. After all, he was Chance McCoy, agent extraordinare. And Hannah Hart, while a delicious diversion, would not come between him and his assignment.

He slowly transformed his expression into his infamous Boris Karloff-Al Capone-Frankenstein look. It had taken several hours of practice in front of a bathroom mirror six years earlier to get the look repulsive enough. This was the look that made even the most hardened of criminals shake with fear. The look that caused women to cross to the other side of the street. The look he knew would not only reduce Hannah to a quivering mass of tears but make her think twice before letting him get close to her again.

"I'm driving home." His voice was authoritative. It was a Chance McCoy, undercover agent, take-charge kind of order.

Her gaze flickered over his face, and she seemed to shrink away. He then made his final, manly declaration. "Okay?"

Did he just ask her if it was okay? Him? He swore under his breath and stalked toward the theater. Chance McCoy didn't ask permission, he gave permission.

"No, it's not okay." She argued all the way to the ticket counter. She kept at it while he bought and paid for the five-minute-old popcorn, which she also told him in no uncertain terms wasn't fresh anymore because he wouldn't get out of the car when she had asked him to. She continued to point out what a great driver she had always been, even after she had found her idea of the perfect seats, and kept at it all the way through the theater's on-screen commercials.

Until he finally turned to her and asked, "Am I going to have to kiss you again to shut you up?"

"Oh! How dare you insult me like that? As if kissing me is something you have to do for punishment. Well, I have news for you, Chance McCoy, you don't have to kiss me to get me to shut up. I can shut up on my own, without your kisses. In fact, I can talk right through your kisses. Why—''

Chance kissed her. Popcorn butter and salt covered her lips, softer and more warm than he would have imagined. And she opened to him, welcoming his deep caress, kissing him back. She reclined in her seat and he moved over her, with only the large bucket of popcorn between them.

Hannah broke the kiss first and he groaned. ''Come here,'' he said. ''I don't want to hear about what a great driver you are.''

''The movie's starting.''

Chance glanced at the screen, then reached for her again. ''It's only a preview.''

''No, it's the feature.''

He watched again for several minutes. ''This isn't the Arnold Schwarzenegger movie.''

''Of course not. I don't think he was acting back in the fifties. It's *Teacher's Pet,* part of the Doris Day film festival.''

Doris Day? What? How had he been so distracted he didn't even know what tickets he had paid for? Hannah reached inside the slightly crushed bucket, brushing his fingers. ''When I was little, I wanted to be Doris Day,'' she whispered.

Chance could have guessed that much. He slouched into the seat, glared at the screen and chomped until a small, satisfied smile crossed his lips. The side of Hannah's full breast felt extremely good against his arm. He relaxed and watched the show.

Clark Gable played a rough newspaper editor. A real man's man. Okay, Chance thought, he could relate to that. Gable was the Schwarzenegger of the forties and fifties.

He smoked and drank and didn't let any dame get in his way.

Then Gable met Doris, gave her a false name and kept his real identity a secret. Not unlike what Chance had to do. In the end, when Doris found out the truth, they lived happily ever after.

Fantasy was fine for Hollywood, but it wouldn't happen in real life. Not in his life.

Then again, if it could happen to Gable…

HANNAH LET CHANCE drive the Tank home from the movies. After all, she knew all about male ego and was a big enough person to let him have his way. They were both surprised to find the Mustang, now painted the original color it had been on his sixteenth birthday, parked in her driveway. Ed must have really felt bad about what he had done to rush the job that much. And Chance wasted no time in getting into the car and taking off with no more than a backward wave in her direction. This was not how she had envisioned the culmination of what had started out as a perfect afternoon.

She heard the phone ringing and ran into the kitchen, snatching the portable off the table.

"Where've you been?" Ada snapped. "I've been calling all afternoon."

"Hello, Hannah, how are you? I'm fine, Mother, and you? Fine, Hannah. And how was your day today? Pleasant, and yours? Just wonderful, dear."

"Don't get testy, Hannah." There was a sliver of hurt under her mother's no-nonsense tone.

Hannah stuck the phone between her shoulder and chin, leaving her hands free to wash the pans from the morning. "I love talking to you every day, but I wish you were calling to be sociable, not to find out if I took my insulin, ate breakfast, checked my glucose level, exercised and whatever else you can think of.''

''I'm your mother. I worry. And I have cause to be concerned.''

It had been twelve months since Ada had found her daughter comatose in the hallway. Hannah knew, even after all that time, her mother still hadn't gotten over the numbing fear of almost losing her only child.

Hannah hadn't meant to stop taking her insulin. She hadn't meant to stop eating. She didn't even realize how depressed she had become after dumb, dead Dave flaunted his disregard for her by getting himself killed in flagrante delicto.

''I promised you a long time ago that Dave won't happen again,'' Hannah softly insisted.

''You're absolutely right,'' Ada sighed. ''I should have said hello first. So, hello.''

''Hello.''

''Now where were you?''

''Oh, Mother.'' It was Hannah's turn to sigh. ''We went to a movie and had a great time.''

That was an understatement. She'd had a romantic adventure. When her hand went into the bucket of popcorn, so did Chance's. When his fingers met hers, she went on fire. And when he took her burning fingers and licked the salt and butter off them slowly, lavishly, she had melted.

''Earth to Hannah. Earth to Hannah.''

''What?''

''You didn't answer my question.''

''What question?''

''I asked who 'he' was?''

''Chance.''

There was a quick intake of breath on the other end.

"Are you planning on seeing him again, in a social sense?"

"I hope so."

"Oh, Hannah," Ada said softly, and Hannah could almost see her mother's head shaking in despair. "I did a terrible thing. I never should have had him move into that apartment. But I didn't think you and Chance would—you know—get along together. He's so Northern and you're so Southern. And he's only temporary."

"He could be permanent with the right incentive." Like her.

"It would never happen."

"Never say never."

"Hannah, listen to your mother. Don't get involved. I don't want to see you hurt again."

Hannah closed her eyes, while the soapy sponge she held circled the bottom of the bowl over and over. The motherly advice had come too late. She was already falling in love.

"Hannah, are you listening to what I'm telling you?"

"Are you pointing your finger at me?"

She could hear her mother's hand slap down on a hard surface. "Never mind that. Forget Chance McCoy. No more movies. No more anything. When his job here is finished, he's leaving, and he won't be sparing you a backward glance."

"You're wrong, Mother." How could she explain that Chance and she were like peanut butter and jelly on homemade buttermilk bread? If they hadn't been, then a kiss would be just a plain old, nothing kiss and not a toecurling, liquefying, tantalizing encounter.

Ada's last words before she hung up were every mother's prophecy. "I'm never wrong."

"Everyone can be wrong once in their life," Hannah mumbled into the dead phone. "Even you."

CHANCE DIDN'T REGRET not seeing Hannah that evening. She was a distraction he didn't need while on this mission. Now, he was certain when his job here was finished, she'd agree to a vacation with him in Cancún. After all, what woman in her right mind wouldn't? Once on the warm beaches in Mexico, she could spend two full weeks distracting him.

Hannah had been right about one thing, though. The way Ed could make a car purr. His drive to the Sugar Land police station in the refurbished Mustang had been the smoothest he'd had in a long time.

Chief Turley had told the desk sergeant that Chance would be using the chief's private computer Sunday evening, so he had a good two hours of uninterrupted time and had finished running the reports sooner than he'd anticipated.

Turley walked in unexpectedly and Chance was glad for the company. Early that morning, before sending the reports to Jim, he'd taken his morning run through several district parks, checking out the buildings and the community areas.

The chief leaned on the edge of the desk. "Did you find anything in particular? Did you get any of those hunches?"

Chance nodded. "I'm getting closer." He gestured to the reports stacked in the middle of the chief's desk. "Those are the records of drug-related offenses in the last five years."

"Not many there."

"No. This town's so clean it squeaks. Never came

across anything quite like it before. Don't you have any dirty laundry hanging out someplace? Anyplace?''

The chief shook his head. "Sugar Land's a pretty good-sized city, with a small-town atmosphere. When I first started to hear mumblings about the town being used as a distribution center for heroin, I couldn't believe it.''

"When did you start believing?''

The chief paced the small room, his hands in his pockets, his keys rattling. "You know we protect our own.''

Chance thought about Hannah and her Hunks, and the rest of her baking, and how the whole city had protected her. He knew the chief wasn't exaggerating.

"We found a truck loaded with heroin on the interstate heading north. Inside the cab was Mac MacNaughton's campaign manager. Shot through the head.''

"MacNaughton's the guy who's running against Ada for mayor.''

"Right. Now, I never liked that weasel, and if anyone could be involved, I'd think it was him. But the truck had been wiped clean.''

"What about MacNaughton?''

"I'd like nothing more than to pin this on him. But his record's clean.''

"You're sure.''

The chief nodded.

"When did the murder happen?''

"Twelve days ago. Then I called Jim, and he sent you.''

"Where's the truck now?''

"In the compound. I'm telling you, though, there's nothing there.''

Chance wished he'd been there when the truck had been found. His sixth sense always worked best at a fresh crime scene. He walked over to the window, hands in his pockets and rocked on the balls of his feet. The blinds were raised and anyone from outside could look up and see the two men clearly. If someone wanted to take a shot, they'd have perfect targets.

Chance went back to the desk and pulled a blank piece of paper toward him. He picked up a pencil and drew a detailed map of the one place he had visited that morning that had sent his sixth sense reeling. "I have a plan."

8

THE NEXT MORNING HANNAH sank into the passenger seat, crossed both arms over her chest in defiance, and without giving a thought to all the Southern manners drilled into her since birth, let out a loud and very unladylike yawn. In further defiance, she didn't hide it behind her hand.

She glanced in Chance's direction, to make sure he'd heard it. He ignored her.

Life didn't seem fair. She always slept late on the second Monday of every month, because she had to spend long hours over the weekend preparing for the Fritz-Simmons sisters' monthly tea party. And because most of the past weekend had been spent either with Chance or thinking about Chance, she had had to stay up later than usual the previous night to finish all the food.

Then, along came Chance, when it was still dark outside, pounding on her back door, although he swore he knocked gently, but she knew a pound when she heard a pound. Woke her up smack in the middle of the dream she'd been having about him, right at the crucial point where he'd been about to make all her fantasies come true. He told her he was giving her a driving lesson which, as far as she was concerned, she didn't need.

"Only milkmen get up this early," she stated through another yawn.

"That so?"

"No, that's not so. Milkmen don't deliver milk in the

mornings anymore. Even they're on a more decent schedule. Probably got themselves better hours through the
milkmen's union."

"Didn't know they had a union."

"What difference does it make?"

"None," he laughed. "Just making conversation."

"Well, don't."

"You started it."

No, he had. No female hormones should have to deal
with a temptation like him, at least not in a Volvo, at five-
thirty in the morning. Especially when the cows didn't
even have to get up this early anymore.

He had his right foot on the accelerator and his leg, bent
at the knee, leaned over toward her. Teasing her. Taunting
her. His thigh muscle bulged through tight washed denim,
and her legs had become warm and tingly as the male heat
of him wafted onto her skin. How dare he purposely make
her sizzle before she'd had her coffee?

"I know why you're doing this," she mumbled sleepily.
"You wanted to see if I look as good in the morning
without makeup as I do after makeup. Well, now you
know. I don't."

"You look fine." He glanced in her direction, scanning
her face. "It's your driving that needs a makeover, not
you."

"I took driver's ed back in high school." She had had
trouble parking back then, too. But there was no reason to
tell Chance that she'd passed the driver's part of the test,
on her third try, because her mother had borrowed the
neighbor's colicky infant and sat with the poor, screaming
baby in the back seat of the car all through the exam. The
examiner passed Hannah and took the rest of the day off
to nurse a migraine.

"That may be your problem," Chance said knowingly. "You've forgotten everything you learned."

"I didn't forget anything. These things just happen to me. You know how it is. Sometimes everything goes along fine, then you have a bad year."

"A bad year? Like a bad-hair day?"

"Exactly. So you do understand." Great, she thought with sorrow. He'd noticed her hair. Well, what did she expect? She'd been lucky she'd convinced him to give her five minutes to shower. He balked at the thought of wasting time so she could blow-dry the wet mass of tangles on top of her head.

"The only thing I understand is that someday you may not back into a parked car. Next time, you might hit a kid."

"I would never let that happen." Hannah glared menacingly at his profile. How dare he even suggest something so horrible? "Never. Not in a million years. I'm too careful."

"The way you drive, I wouldn't be too sure."

"You're mistaking the way I park for the way I drive. I drive very well—I park terribly."

Chance turned the Volvo down Sweetwater Boulevard. "Have you forgotten I was with you yesterday?"

"You made me nervous. I told you that. I'm not normally that scattered."

He glanced at her, disbelief evident in his expression.

"I only agreed to come out with you at this ungodly hour, anyway, because you're lonely," she mumbled under her breath.

"What did you say?"

"Nothing."

"Repeat it."

She did.

He swore, gripping the wheel tighter.

Now that she brought the subject up, she figured she had nothing to lose by continuing. "It's not that I mind being the one to fill up your hours, but still, let's be honest with each other. You know and I know we're together this morning for a reason, and it has nothing to do with driving lessons." She smoothed her hands down her bare thighs. His gaze followed her movement.

"So, Chance, be honest and admit you seek out my company. Hey! Look where you're going."

Chance slammed on the brakes halfway through a stop sign.

Hannah sniffed self-righteously. "See?"

"You're purposely trying to distract me."

"No, I'm not." She drummed her fingers on her knee-cap.

Chance focused his gaze on her hand and knee as he turned into the parking lot of Clements High School. The right tire jumped the curb. "Don't say one word."

She turned her face away and grinned in silence.

Chance took a deep, exasperated breath, put the car in park, and with the engine idling, opened the door. "We've got an hour before the kids start arriving for school. Switch places with me."

Hannah slid over to the seat that he had vacated, closed the door, put the car in drive and drove off. She heard him yelling and watched in the rearview mirror as he waved his hands above his head.

"God," she murmured. "You are truly one magnificent specimen."

Hannah made a perfect circle around the perimeter of the parking lot before pulling up next to where Chance stood, fuming. His hands were shoved into the front pockets of his jeans, which caused the fabric to mold tightly over all his male muscles.

"You took off without me." His lips were set in a grim line.

She licked hers. "You know, Chance, I've been thinking." Hannah rested her arm on the window frame and looked up into his face. And what a face.

"Why am I suddenly worried?"

"I don't know. Why are you? It just doesn't make sense to me. I've never had a ticket. I've never been stopped for speeding. I've got a perfectly clean driving record. In fact, all my records are clean. Are yours?"

"What do you mean?"

"Well, a girl can't be too careful anymore. Now I know I have no social diseases, unless you want to count diabetes. But diabetes is only a social disease when I can't have sweets at a party, which some people, especially those who want to fatten me up, think is antisocial. But I know I don't have AIDS or herpes, or syphilis or gonorrhea, or even pinkeye, for that matter. What about you?"

Chance's look of surprise slowly transformed into a devastatingly roguish grin. Her blood rushed through her veins, pounded into her heart and sent juices flowing in places she longed for him to touch.

"I work for the city, don't I?" he answered. "Do you think they would have hired me if I weren't healthy? In every way?"

"Well, well. Happy days are here again," she murmured softly. Then, louder... "I'll tell you what I'm going to do."

"No." He held his hand up. "I'll tell you. Move over and I'll take you home."

"No, no, no, no." Hannah shook her head and finger at the same time. "I am going to stay right here in this position and let you in the passenger side. And then I'm going to drive you, very carefully, over to the Pancake House.''

"I have to get to work."

"You have to eat breakfast, and I have to eat. I'm on a tight schedule, as far as my food intake goes." She looked into his eyes, to see if that bothered him. Dave had hated her schedule.

"I planned on grabbing a doughnut on my way to the park."

Hannah reached out and captured his hand in hers, turned it over and ran her fingernail down the finely etched lines of his palm. "Doughnuts are good, but I can't eat a doughnut. I was thinking along the lines of scrambled egg whites with toast, a double order of bacon, crisp, and a fresh, hot cup of coffee. What do you think about that?"

Chance followed the mesmerizing movement of her fingers. "Can you get there without killing us?"

"Has your life flashed before your eyes today?"

He shook his head.

"There's your answer."

He walked around the other side of the car and thought about how much sense Hannah's logic seemed to be making.

It was already past six in the morning by the time they were seated at the restaurant. Waitresses ran up and down the aisles, their arms loaded down with food and carafes. Chance nursed his coffee. Hannah downed hers in three gulps, then said, "Now we can talk about the plans."

"What plans?"

"For the team."

"What team?"

"Remember you said you'd be the head coach for the Angels?"

"I could never forget that." He had forgotten and now that he remembered, he wished she had forgotten.

She picked up the carafe and poured more coffee into her cup. "Great kids, all between the ages of six and eight."

"Kids?" He knew he didn't agree to anything having to do with kids. Next thing he knew, she'd have him walking a dog or something. "That wasn't part of our deal."

"What are you talking about? Of course, it was. You agreed to be head coach."

The waitress set the food on the table and left. "I thought this was a women's team. Hannah, I don't know the first thing about kids. But I know a lot about women. Me and kids have nothing in common. They're younger than me. And short."

"They won't always be short."

He glared at her.

"Well, they won't," she insisted.

"Maybe they won't, but I still can't. Listen, I'm going to tell you a secret. Something I've never told anyone before. My one and only flaw."

"Oh, Chance." Hannah reached out and patted his hand. "You can share all your flaws with me."

"I never played baseball."

"That's great." She sounded triumphant. "It's better if you don't know anything. Then, there won't be too many of your bad habits to get rid of." She reached inside her handbag and pulled out a thick paperback, entitled, *Children's Baseball: Everything You Need to Know.* "Here, read this. It'll be very helpful. Everything you'll need is right here in this little book."

"Little?" It weighed at least five pounds.

"That's only Volume One. I don't think you'll need

Volume Two. Now, remember, there will be parents there who'll want to help guide you, too.''

"I'll need all the help I can get."

"But not from them. They'll shout at you, swear at you, browbeat you—"

"That won't work."

"Of course, it won't." She reached inside her purse and handed him two tiny rubber stoppers. "Because you'll be wearing these. Earplugs. They work wonders at blocking out parents. You don't want to hear what they're saying, anyway. Parents are always so negative. It'll color your outlook on human nature."

Chance stared at the delicate woman with the big heart. She wanted to make the world a better place and she had just confessed that her efforts to help the kids she cared so much about were unappreciated. "Why are you going to all this trouble? It's not as if you don't have anything else going on in your life."

"The league was short one manager. If I didn't do it, no one else would have. My Angels were the kids not good enough to be picked in the first-, second- or even third-round draft for the teams that had already formed. If I didn't do this, they wouldn't be able to play."

If he made any objection to coaching now, after her confession, he'd look like a creep. "All right. Knowing that my knowledge is limited, what do you want me to do?"

"Oh, I'm sure you know a lot more than you think you know," Hannah said enthusiastically. "Tomorrow night, we have our first practice at Sugar Land Park Number Six. Do you know where that is?"

His hash browns were suspended in midair as he quickly looked up into her face. That was the park where his sixth sense had overflowed. "Yes."

"Great. This weekend is the annual Sugar Land Faire, which is held right in front of the sugar factory. Now the Faire is very, very important, because it awards the only trophy our team has a chance of winning this year. It has nothing to do with skills on the baseball field and everything to do with creativity."

"What do you do?"

"All the teams in the league are in charge of a booth, and they make exhibits. The theme, this year, is Our Sweet Past. The Royal Sugar Company has made up these really incredible commemorative sugar boxes for the league to sell for fund-raisers this year. Which is a lot better than selling candy like we've done for the past six years, if you ask me. I'm going to use the sugar boxes, which I'm sure no one will mind. But just in case someone does, I'm keeping the project a secret—except for telling you and the kids."

Chance was getting short of breath listening to her talk.

"We'll use the sugar boxes like bricks and we'll build a replica of the old Sugar Land city hall. It'll be wonderful."

"Are you sure you need my help?" His talents were in other areas.

"I really do need you."

She gave him *that* look. Oh, he knew that look all right. It was the one that said, "If you take on this job you'll be my hero. If you don't, you're scum." Chance watched Hannah munch daintily on her toast, all dewy-eyed and innocent. He leaned over the table, and with the pad of his thumb, he brushed a dusting of crumbs off her chin. Her chewing slowed and her lips parted slightly; a blush started at her freckled cheeks and blossomed.

He really didn't have a choice in the matter. He hadn't

been around a lot of blushing women. He wanted to be her hero.

AFTER BREAKFAST CHANCE took Hannah and her Tank back home, got in the Shelby and drove directly to Sugar Land District Park Number Six. The first time he'd been to this park was the previous morning. Then, he'd come back with Chief Turley late last night, using the map he'd drawn up to outline his plan visually.

Chance had been through every district park in the city at least once since he had arrived the previous Friday. But none except Park Number Six, had made his sixth sense tremble.

Just to test his hunches one final time, to make sure he had himself in working order, he slowly circled the first building, the one Turley called the field house. He didn't feel any twinges, which was a good sign.

In the distance, he could see four baseball fields and the concession stand, which had been built as a smaller version of the field house. He took his time heading in that direction, and just like the previous morning and again that night, the closer he came to the concession stand, the stronger the current of electricity that ran through him.

When he finally stood directly in front of the building, the muscles in his temples began to pound. The throbbing was even stronger now than it had been the night before.

Chance walked slowly around the building. He stopped to pick up an empty soda can, and while bending over, he felt for the gun strapped to his ankle. Straightening, taking the can with him, he continued around the building. Every instinct told him he was getting closer. He had always felt euphoric when he came this close to capturing his prey. Only, now, for the first time, he felt a sense of loss. He knew his time in Sugar Land would soon end. But, hell, he'd known that from the beginning. He never thought this job would last more than a week. Two at tops.

Chance stopped in front of the concession-stand door, which now stood propped open by an industrial-size waste barrel. The previous night, the same door had been shut tight and locked. Turley had unlocked it and they had gone inside together. And that's when Chance knew he had found what he'd come to Sugar Land to find.

"Hello," he called out, throwing the can in the barrel, taking two steps inside the building. "Anyone in here?"

A man yelled from deeper inside, "Coming."

Chance didn't have to wait long.

The slender man who came toward him, holding Laser Lightning Sugar Smackeroos in his hand, said, "Don't I remember you from the party the other night? Chance Mc-Coy, right? I'm Elvin Evans."

Chance's blood level shot up, sweat formed on his forehead and his vision momentarily blurred. "You're Hannah's insurance agent."

"Right. Hannah's really something. Nine accidents this year already."

"She told me," Chance said, knowing she still hadn't told Elvin about number ten.

"She's nothing, if not honest." Elvin looked at him slyly. "Not to get personal, but rumor has it you're living with her."

Where were these people coming up with that story? "Not with her. In the garage apartment behind the house."

"So, she finally rented that place. On a professional level, I have to say that's too bad, because now her homeowner's insurance premium will be lower. You know— less commission. On a personal level, well, what can I say?" Elvin threw the candy on the counter, stuck his hands in his pockets and got a sheepish grin on his face.

"Hannah and I, well, she's kind of wonderful, if you know what I mean." He waggled his eyebrows and winked.

"No. What do you mean?" Chance knew exactly what the rat meant. He had to control his hands, which had already formed into fists, to keep them from connecting with Elvin's big nose.

"I've loved her since we were in third grade. But, hell, so did every other guy. Only she never got serious about any of us hometown boys. I thought all was lost forever, but luckily Dave got himself killed, so I'm kind of hoping, now that I'm divorced and free, well, maybe I'll have a chance with her."

Over his dead body, Chance seethed. Instead, he said politely, "They just don't make women like Hannah anymore."

Elvin nodded. "When they made her, they stopped production on that model. I'm going to do the only right thing and marry her. Of course, Peter loves her, too."

"Peter?" Why didn't these guys take a number? Stand in line? Get a life? Preferably in a different state.

"My son. He'd give anything to have Hannah as his stepmother."

"I bet he would." What was it with that woman? Maybe he should consider himself lucky he'd be leaving town before she made him fall madly, deeply and forever in love with her, too, just like these saps.

"And I have to say, that as a wife, well, you know what they say about redheaded women. They're hot. Which makes up for her cooking, if you know what I mean." He elbowed Chance in the ribs and winked.

"Yeah. Hot." Elvin's face might have turned red, but it was Chance's blood pressure that skyrocketed even higher than it had when he had entered the concession stand. Now he couldn't tell if the sharp stabs he had felt inside him had to do with Elvin and heroin or Elvin and wanting to punch his lights out. He took a deep breath and cleared his mind, focusing completely on the man in front of him and not the woman he had dropped off an hour before. "What are you stocking in there?"

"Food. Come on. I'll show you the storage room."

Chance followed him through the building and into a small room built off the main area. Last night the storage room had been empty, but now it was a quarter of the way stocked with boxes of food and beverages.

"We open for business the first day of baseball season. Our major fund-raising drive this year is selling Royal sugar in commemorative boxes. All profits go toward uniforms and equipment."

Elvin took the only two boxes of Royal sugar off the shelf and placed them on the counter. "I bought those for me to take home. I have to make brownies for Peter's Cub Scout troop."

The box had been designed to look like a replica of the sugar factory. "Like the packaging."

"Nice isn't it. Royal Sugar designed them especially for the league. They won't be sold anywhere else."

"Can I see one?"

With barely a moment's hesitation, Elvin handed a box to Chance. And Chance's fingers burned so hot he almost dropped it. He might have had hunches before, but he now had confirmation that his sixth sense had directed him, once again, to the right place. "When's the rest come in?"

Elvin shrugged. "Not sure. A couple of days, I guess."

Chance knew Elvin could pinpoint the exact time those sugar boxes would be delivered. And he also knew he'd be here waiting. "Do you mind if I take a box to Hannah? She's out."

"Sorry, no can do." Elvin shook his head regretfully.

"I need both of them. The grocery store is open twenty-four hours, though, if you're desperate. Wish I could help."

"You have. More than you know," Chance said on his way out.

He stopped by the police station on his way home to tell the chief about meeting Elvin. When he finally got back to the apartment, he phoned Jim and requested more detailed information on Elvin, Mac MacNaughton and Henry Perkins, the man found dead in the white truck. Now the waiting began. And Chance had never claimed to be a patient man.

He paced the small apartment, peering through the kitchen window at least a dozen times, looking for something—or someone—and not finding it. Finally, he stripped off his jeans and T-shirt and headed for the shower.

HANNAH HADN'T REALLY thought Chance would come to the Fritz-Simmonses' tea party. When he said he'd probably make it, she figured he was only being polite, saying what he thought she wanted to hear.

Hannah knew the moment Chance arrived. Millie Fritz-Simmons came bustling into the kitchen twittering like a june bug about "Hannah's young man."

Chance followed Mattie, Millie's twin sister, into the kitchen, and Hannah, taking one look at him, knew exactly why Millie twittered and figured she herself would melt right then and there. And she would have, too, except the sisters had told her to prepare the tea party for fifty women. And they always underestimated the numbers. She had been catering Millie and Mattie's monthly Sugar Land Ladies of Society tea for the past two years and knew to prepare for at least ten more. Only this time seventy had shown up, so she was scrambling, frantically making more cream-cheese-and-pineapple sandwiches, when Chance had walked in.

"I like your jeans," Hannah said, hardly sparing him more than a fifth glance, because she knew if she looked at him one more time, she'd drop everything and drag him upstairs to an empty bedroom.

"Thanks." He leaned against the counter, giving her the once-over. "I like your, ah, what is it?"

"Dress."

"Of course. Where are your legs?"

"Under the dress."

He reached out for the hem and she scooted away. "I think you're lying. There are no legs under there."

"If you want to see legs, you're going to have to work for the privilege."

"I'm at your service." And he bowed regally.

And she had a real struggle to stop herself from walking around behind him and asking him to repeat the bow, so she could fill up on the view of very tight buttocks molded beneath very tight jeans. Chance took the silver tray Hannah had filled with tiny, delicate sandwiches and listened carefully as she gave him directions to where the Fritz-Simmonses put their tea-party guests. Considering the directions came from Hannah, they were really pretty good. She had said, "Follow the noise."

The chattering got louder the closer he came to the back-yard. A green-and-white striped tent had been set up in the carefully tended azalea garden. Chance placed the tray in an empty space on the buffet table, near other trays loaded with tiny quartered sandwiches, all crusts removed and filled with a variety of centers such as salmon, watercress, cucumbers and now the cream-cheese-and-pineapple he had brought in.

The women drank orange iced tea from Waterford goblets and sipped hot Earl Grey out of bone china cups with a flowered pattern.

Serving the women were Hannah's part-time employees, Beverly and Lois, whom he recognized from the dessert party the other night. The guests were dressed in afternoon frocks of colorful, pastel chiffon flowers and wore big straw hats decorated with flowers, ribbons, bows and a few stuffed birds. Most wore white cotton gloves clasped at the wrists with pearl buttons. What stunned him, though, was seeing the women actually *eating* the food. He hadn't expected that. No one chucked away anything in a garbage can, flowerpot or handbag. They were actually chewing and swallowing.

The party had almost reached the end, when Chance finally made it back to the kitchen and Hannah. The first thing she asked him was, "Are they eating the desserts?"

"There's hardly a pastry left."

"Good. I was so worried. I have a confession to make," she whispered even though they were alone in the kitchen. "It's about the chocolate éclairs and strawberry tarts. I had to buy them at the French bakery. I feel terrible. I had planned on making them yesterday, but you and I went to the movies. I hope the Fritz-Simmonses won't mind. I did bring the Hunks."

"I don't think they'll notice." That explained why the desserts had disappeared. "Did you make the sandwiches?" If she hadn't, that would also explain the rush for nourishment.

"I made everything else. I even baked the bread. We have the parties down to a science. Beverly does all the flower arrangements and Lois is the one who puts together the teas, tables and napkins. They both serve, too. I make the sandwiches, most of the desserts and arrange the trays.

I don't think Hannah's Hunks would have been as successful as it is without Bev and Lois, though. This is a team operation.''

"Whatever you're doing works. The women at this party seem satisfied. They're smiling.''

"I hate to disillusion you, but this crowd would smile over beef jerky. They like to pretend they're the tea-party set, but I've been around them all my life and I know the truth.''

"And their secrets are safe with you, I'll bet.'' Chance leaned against the counter and ran his finger from her wrist to the bend in her elbow. She shivered under his touch. "Can I feed you a little sugar?'' he asked.

"I don't eat sugar.''

He cupped her chin, rubbing the delicate bone with his thumb, before the need to taste her overcame him. "But I do.'' He feathered kisses near the corner of her mouth, then slowly nibbled a path around her chin...and jaw...and neck, until he reached her ear.

Her vanilla perfume enticed him, taunted him, made him wish for everything forbidden to a man like him. She moaned, deep in her throat, turned her head until her mouth and his were together and captured his lips with her own, sucking, licking, straining closer, deeper.

"Hannah.'' Mattie Fritz-Simmons came bustling into the kitchen. "Oh my,'' she exclaimed and turned to leave again.

"Wait!'' Hannah broke away, and with an embarrassed smile, she said, "Don't go, Mattie. What can I get you?''

"I only wanted to ask if you could leave those little cucumber sandwiches, if there's any left. For dinner tonight.''

"I always leave you everything that's left over.''

"I know, dear." Mattie glanced slyly at Chance. "Are you leaving him, too?"

"He's not a leftover."

Mattie sighed. "You seemed so preoccupied, sister and I were hoping you'd forget he was here and give us more experienced girls a chance at happiness."

Hannah hugged Mattie, smiled at Chance and went back to packing her supplies, as if he were already forgotten. Would Hannah forget him when he left Sugar Land? He hadn't thought her capable of forgetting someone as unforgettable as he was. But over the past two hours, his vision of who Hannah really was had made a rapid 360-degree turn. She couldn't bake, that was true, but, given time, she'd learn. And he knew, now, she really was perfectly capable of taking take care of herself. She didn't need him. He should be rejoicing. He could leave town without so much as a backward glance. So he why did he have this empty feeling in the pit of his stomach?

9

"OH, YEAH, BABY. You're doing just fine," Chance murmured, stroking the Shelby's dashboard as he drove back to Sugar Land District Park Number Six at exactly six o'clock on Tuesday evening for his first coaching experience. "That's it, sweetheart. Keep purring." Nothing compared with riding in the Mustang. He knew exactly what she was going to do and when. He could anticipate her every move.

Not like Hannah, whom he spotted the moment he turned into the parking lot. Hard to miss her. She seemed very tall when surrounded by a bunch of knee-high runts.

All right. He admitted to himself she made him crazy with desire. Hard to deny it, when his body hardened at the mere thought of her. Every single time he saw her long legs, slender hips, full breasts and fiery hair, his heart palpitated and his mouth went dry. He hoped Hannah knew artificial resuscitation. With his heart going crazy like it was, he might pass out and need to be revived.

Hannah watched Chance climb out of the car and she whispered under her breath, "Well, I'll be." The children turned, one by one, to look toward where she stared. Fourteen pairs of eyes zeroed in on the bright red Mustang. The fifteenth pair, Hannah's, were dead center on the driver.

Chance saluted them, and the children waved back. Hannah tried to lift her arm, but it had turned to jelly.

He grabbed the bottom of his shirt and pulled the material over his head. From this distance, she could still see the smile he sent her way.

"My-oh-my," she breathed out. She had known he was hot. Didn't she need to fan herself whenever he stood near? Didn't she have to concentrate on not fainting when he kissed her? But never in her wildest dreams did she imagine that her hormones would go into overdrive with only one look at his bare chest.

He walked around the car, which by itself, shouldn't have made her pant. But when he took his shirt and rubbed the hood, she had to restrain herself from running over, laying herself on top of the red steel and begging for the same treatment.

When he lifted his arm and those biceps bulged, it was perfectly natural that she needed ice water. But, oh, Lord, his pectorals had her drooling. They flexed and pulled and rotated his arms in toward his body as he bent over the Shelby's cherry-red finish to rub the hood in slow, rhythmic circles.

And she knew exactly why he did it, all that bending over and rubbing around. To drive her crazy with desire.

Hannah clutched the clipboard, her head held high, baseball cap on straight, and walked purposefully over to where he flexed. The children followed.

"You're not in uniform." She pointed to his belly button. An *ini*e.

"Yes I am."

"You're naked."

He chuckled. "I'm wearing the four S's. Shirt, shorts, shoes and socks."

"You are not wearing a shirt."

He held it up. His biceps blossomed. "Here it is."

Her heart pounded. "Put it on."

"It's hot out."

He didn't have to tell her that. She was sweating. "You have to be presentable for the children."

He laughed. "Look around you."

She turned. All the boys had taken off their shirts, tying the sleeves in knots around their waists. The girls were calling out, "No fair, no fair."

"Put your shirt back on," she hissed at Chance, turned to the children and repeated the instructions. They grumbled, but complied.

"You're making a big deal about nothing." Chance gave her a cocky grin.

He was half right. She was making a big deal, but it wasn't about nothing. Not when the look he gave her said, "I want to take your clothes off slowly and nibble every place that's not tan, and lick you and kiss you and suck you until you're depleted and I'm depleted, and then start all over again." She needed water. Fast.

The waistband of his jeans was slung low, revealing about an inch and a half of boxers. Although she told herself she wasn't really looking where those boxer shorts were peeking through, one couldn't help but see that they had hearts on them. Hearts for her, Hannah Hart.

Oh, yes, her mother had been wrong. Very wrong. The proof was right there on his underwear. Chance didn't have to say, "Hannah Hart, you have my heart." His boxers did that for him. Big hearts, little hearts and winking hearts. Hearts winking at her meant something. If Chance didn't wear his heart on his sleeve, then he certainly wore it over a place she had come to greatly admire. And apparently, after another quick glance in that direction, he admired her, too.

Poor Chance. He might think Sugar Land was temporary, that he would go on to bigger and better parks, but she knew once he had her, he'd never let her go. Now all she had to do was make sure he had her.

She blew her whistle hard and yelled, "Follow me, team," and marched away, not sparing Chance, his chest or his winking hearts a backward glance.

Chance watched her walk away and prided himself on the stiff control he had over all his urges. And the very fact that he could control the baser urge of his maleness to mate with her femaleness gave him power and strength. Which he needed now, more than ever, as he followed Hannah and her munchkins toward the baseball field.

The parade halted at a grassy patch near the concession stand. Hannah's green Jansport backpack, several bulging navy duffel bags with bats sticking out of the tops, a red cooler and a thirty-three-gallon green trash can filled to the top with baseballs were set off to the side.

The kids sat on the grass in a circle that was more oblong than round. She brought the backpack over to them and pulled out a plastic container filled with yellow paste.

"Okay, kids." She knelt down to their level, her derriere resting on her heels.

He admired that about her. The derriere. On anyone else, it would be nothing but a butt. Hannah's though deserved a fancier term because it was so—he bent his head to the left, squinted his eyes to focus better and crossed his arms—fancy.

"You all understand that we're going to build a replica of the old Sugar Land city hall with the sugar boxes."

The Angels nodded.

"Chance." She turned around and caught him midstare. A gold locket swung from her neck and twinkled in the sunlight. So did Hannah's smile. "Will you please run inside there and bring out six boxes of sugar? The commemorative ones. Do you know what I'm talking about?"

"I was here yesterday and saw Elvin, Hannah. The sugar hadn't been delivered yet."

"It's here now. I was just in there and the place is stocked full of it."

Two things ran though Chance's mind as he walked slowly toward the concession stand. The first and more important one was that his hunches hadn't given him so much as a tweak since he'd arrived at the park. His brain had been so busy thinking about Hannah in shorts, he hadn't even asked himself why. And second, if heroin was in the sugar boxes, as he suspected, his time remaining in Sugar Land had, for all intents, just ended.

Hannah had left the door to the concession stand unlocked. One step inside, and the familiar bolt of lightning rammed through him. He flipped on the light switch and glanced around, his heart hammering wildly in his chest.

Pay dirt. Cartons were everywhere, some sealed shut, others open. Hundreds of them. Mountains of heroin all dressed up in commemorative sugar boxes. Elvin had been here already, too. He had left his inventory sheet, along with destination codes. Arrogant little twerp. Only someone so sure of not getting caught would be this careless.

"Coach Chance." One of the kids from the team ran into the building and halted. "Wow! Mountains."

"Seems like it. What do you need?"

"Coach Hannah told me to come and find you. She thinks you got lost."

"I'm coming right now." Chance pulled six sugar boxes from a carton, his fingers burning with each one he touched, and left the building, locking the door behind him.

The closer he got to Hannah, the cooler his fingers became. Two feet from her and all his twinges disappeared.

The boxes of sugar felt exactly like boxes of sugar. Nothing evil or sinister. And he felt fear.

"Of course, since we don't know what the old City Hall looked like, or even if there was one, we can really use our imagination," Hannah was saying. "We've been given booth number..." she glanced at her clipboard "...ten."

Taking the sugar from Chance, she said to the kids, "Here's the plan. Inside this plastic container is a kind of magic glue that doesn't make things stick together permanently." She took the lid off and dipped her finger inside the yellow goop. "If you take a little dot like this—" she put a small blot on one box "—then put the other box on top if it, it sticks." She held the two boxes, now stuck together, up in the air.

"We're going to use our share of the fund-raising boxes to build the replica, and we can sell any boxes we don't use at the fair. The only thing is, we can't use any more than our allotment, which is twenty-five boxes each."

Hannah handed the boxes back to Chance and he almost felt sorry for her. There would be no model made out of these sugar boxes. He hoped she had an alternative plan.

"On the day of the Faire, I want you all here by eight in the morning, and if you can, bring your parents to help. Okay?"

They all nodded.

"Any questions?" She waited a few seconds, before saying, "No! Great. Let's practice."

She looked at Chance. "I'm going to do you a big favor, since you don't have any experience with children."

"Thanks."

"You're welcome. Vicki and Trish are the Angels' pitchers. And Peter and Chucky are learning how to be catchers. So they all go together. Why don't you take them over there." Hannah pointed to a large, grassy area near the parking lot. "I'll stay here with the rest of the team, and practice inside the fenced field. That way you won't have to be overwhelmed."

He glanced down at the two skinny, little girls who couldn't have weighed more than forty pounds each, their throwing arms no larger in size than a number-two pencil. Neither kid had teeth. "Are you telling me *they* are your pitchers? Do you think I was born yesterday?"

"You'll have to trust me on this." Hannah smiled.

Women. He gave up. Try and reason with them, and what did he get? A *trust me.* "All right, Hannah. But don't expect miracles." He looked down at the four kids entrusted to his care. Baby-sitting. The thought made him cringe. "Let's go."

He carried one of the blue duffel bags and they took off. "Hannah made a mistake." He dropped the bag, put his hands on his hips and scanned the area assigned to them.

"No, she didn't," Chucky said. "We practice out here all the time. See." He pointed to the where the grass had been trodden into a baseball diamond.

Yes, it was a field all right. Now what? "I'll be right back. I need to get something from the car. Don't move," he ordered.

Chance jogged over to the Shelby, reached inside and grabbed the five-pound instruction book. When he got back to the kids, they were still in the same place he had left them. "All right. Sit down, everyone. We're going to have a baseball review."

Chance flipped open to chapter one, skimmed the page, then paraphrased, "Rule number one—know the equipment." He reached inside the duffel bag and pulled out a rubber base. "What's this?" He held it over his head.

"A base," four voices chirped.

"Great. You guys passed the first quiz. Rule number two—know the purpose. What's it used for?"

"You're supposed to kick it with your foot and run around all of them until you get to home plate. Then you win," Vicki said.

"You don't win, you get a run," Trish corrected. "Only stupid Peter here never kicks the base, he always jumps over them, and then he gets out."

"Don't call me stupid." Peter pushed Trish on the shoulder and she pushed back.

"Stop it, both of you," Chance barked.

They stopped.

"What happens if you don't hit the base when you're running?"

"The next time you're up, you get to hit it twice," Peter answered.

The others nodded.

Chance scowled, flipping to "Chapter Three, Basic Rules," and read out loud about the consequences of not touching the base. When he got to the end of the page, he looked up. The kids were blowing and popping saliva bubbles. "Have you been listening to me?"

"Huh?" they asked together.

Chance swore under his breath. "All right, everyone get up."

They rose.

"I'm hot," Chucky said.

"I'm tired," Trish complained.

"I want to go home," Vicki moaned.

"Get a grip, kiddos." Chance glared at each one. "This is baseball. Learn to spit."

A great slurping noise came out of the four pip-squeaks. Then they spat. Saliva landed on grass and shoes. Slick moisture hung down their chins. They wiped their mouths with the backs of their hands and looked up at him expectantly.

"Hey!" Chance's eyes flicked from one kid to the next. "I'm impressed."

Their little mouths split into the widest, most toothless grins he'd ever seen. Tiny shoulders lifted with pride. They stood proud and tall. Well, as tall as four-footers could stand.

"My first impression of you was all wrong. You all have what it takes to be great baseball players. It's in the spit. Okay, team, take these bases and space them out." He handed each a square. "We'll practice throwing, catching and hitting the bases with your feet when you run. Who wants to pitch first?"

"I do." Vicki jumped up and down, her hand raised.

"Do you know how to throw?"

"Of course." She looked at him with utter disdain.

Chance shrugged. "Trish, do you want to catch, and then Peter and Chucky can take turns at bat."

The four children took their places. Trish had her back to the parking lot, Vicki stood on the pitcher's mound facing Trish, and Chucky had a bat in his hand, looking determined. Chance stood off to the side.

Vicki wound her arm, like a crank, several times, then threw. The ball only made it halfway to the batter, and Trish ran out to pick it up.

"That's okay." Chance didn't want Vicki to get discouraged.

She looked over at him, smiled toothlessly and gave him the thumbs-up sign, which he returned. She again cranked her arm, rotating faster and faster before letting the ball fly.

Chance watched it sail over all the kids' heads, past the

field and right smack through the windshield of his Shelby, breaking a hole dead center.

His mouth dropped to the grass. Vicki's gloved hand covered half her face, but not her saucer-wide eyes. There were several awe-inspired "wows" a couple of "cools" and two or three "awesomes."

Vicki began to sob so hard her tiny body shook. Chance knelt down until he was eye level with her.

"Are you gonna tell on me?" she whispered fearfully.

"No. No, I'm not."

"I didn't mean to hit your car."

"It can be fixed." He couldn't believe he'd said that. Since when had he, Chance McCoy, become a marshmallow? He didn't offer comfort to munchkins. Especially munchkins who wrecked his car.

"Do you hate me now?"

"Are you kidding? With an arm like that? Even I know your arm is special. Why you're going to be our ringer."

"I don't want to ring bells, Coach."

"That's not what I mean. You're going to be the one nobody would suspect to be the star of the show. The person who takes the team to the playoffs. The championship."

She hiccuped. "Oh. So it's good, then."

He put his arm around her tiny shoulders. "It's the best." And he felt deep regret knowing he wouldn't be around to see it happen.

10

HANNAH GENTLY ROLLED the first vial of insulin between her palms, mixing the liquid. She stuck the needle through the rubber stopper, withdrew fluid, then tapped the plastic barrel several times, getting rid of air bubbles before inserting the needle into the second insulin vial. She sterilized a small area on her thigh, then injected the shot.

She had just put the vials away, discarded the used syringe and finished off the cheese sandwich when the school bell on the veranda began to clang. Chance's timing, as always, was perfect.

The moment Hannah opened the front door and saw him standing there, his hair still wet from a recent shower and enticingly disheveled, his faded jeans molded to hips, her heart began to race. His white T-shirt had been tucked into the waistband of the jeans, accentuating the muscular planes of his chest, the slimness of his hips, the flatness of his belly. Over it he was wearing a long-sleeved plaid shirt in shades of red and blue, unbuttoned, shirttails hanging.

Chance leaned a muscled shoulder on the door frame, held a bottle of wine in one hand and a bouquet of flowers in the other.

Hannah stood back, giving him space to enter. "I'm sorry about what happened to your car."

"You apologized this afternoon." A pained look crossed his face. "I don't blame you for the windshield."

"I know. But I still feel somewhat responsible. I wanted to also thank you for being so nice to Vicki and the other kids. Getting them candy and letting them help you clean up the glass."

"I'm a nice guy." His dangerous grin proclaimed the opposite. "That's why, when you invited me over tonight for a pot-roast dinner, I said to myself, 'Myself,' I said, 'sure I'll go to Hannah's house for an evening of edible pleasure. What could possibly happen to me that hasn't already happened? My teeth have already survived her cookies. My Shelby will make a remarkable comeback from her tortured condition. My body has been in a state of tense anticipation ever since I arrived in town. And now Hannah is extending an invitation to partake in some tender and juicy cuisine. There's no way any man in his right mind would refuse a woman who's so easy on the palate and erotic to the senses.'"

"Exactly." Hannah beamed. "And thank you for the wine and flowers. They're beautiful." She buried her nose in the bouquet.

"Fresh from your garden. Those," he pointed to the orange mums and marigolds, "reminded me of your hair."

She automatically touched her curls and her fingers snagged. "My hair's red."

"I know. The flowers have six different shades."

"I guess that explains it." No wonder he thought she couldn't cook. The man was color-blind.

Chance followed her to the kitchen and waited next to the sink, watching her fill a vase with water and arrange the flowers.

He had a magical power over her senses. Her insides had melted to liquid putty, blood pounded in her ears, her fingertips seemed numb one moment and sensitive to every touch the next. "I haven't started the roast, yet. I thought

I'd wait until you got here, so I could show you exactly what I do.''

He pressed the small of his back against the counter, crossed his arms in front of him and looked in the direction where her breasts should have been, if they hadn't been covered by the apron.

"Pay attention," she scolded.

He slowly raised his potent gaze. "I'm yours."

If only that were really true. She cleared her throat. "On the counter I have all the ingredients needed to make Hannah Hart's Heavenly Haven."

She swept her hand in the direction of the meat and vegetables. "Which is more commonly known as pot roast. Now, presentation is everything. So, in order for me to prepare a pot roast to perfection, I can't be rushed." She fluttered her lashes. Chance seemed hypnotized by the movement, so she fluttered some more. "Are you in a hurry?"

He blinked away the glazed look and shook his head, reaching for her hand. Her skin tingled under his light touch.

"Have you ever made pot roast?" she asked.

"I've roasted one or two in my life."

"I just bet you have." Hannah pulled her hand out of his grasp, then touched his strong, arrogant chin with her fingertips.

His eyes burned at her touch. Her mouth became sandy and dry, which she realized was a good sign since it meant nature, in its infinite wisdom, had already transferred the moisture in her mouth to more needy portions of her body. "Some people like me are just natural talents in the kitchen. I'm giving you the benefit of years of study. What you'll get tonight is perfection," she told him.

"Perfection worries me." Chance pushed a curl behind her ear, cupping the side of her face in his hand.

"It shouldn't." She leaned into his palm, then immediately backed away.

"If I get used to perfection, I may never be satisfied with mediocrity again."

"Exactly my point." She finger-brushed his hair away from his forehead. "You shouldn't have to." She took in a deep breath, and continued in a schoolteacher voice. "Hannah Hart's Heavenly Haven is an exact science. Did you know that preparation is also extremely important? More important than presentation?"

"No, but I'm sure you'll explain."

"That's what I'm here for. You'll have to pay close attention. I never do the same thing twice. Do you promise?"

He smiled that devilish grin again. "Promise."

"Watch carefully now."

He watched. All parts of her.

Now Hannah smiled. "First you have to peel the carrots, very slowly, so that you get all the skin."

"Get all the skin." He nodded.

"You take potatoes and scrub them clean. Unlike a carrot, potato skin is good to eat. That's where all the vitamins and minerals are. You want to make sure you eat plenty of potatoes."

He made noncommittal noises.

"Then you take celery and onions and chop them very finely. This will ensure that all the aromatic flavors are used to their best advantage."

Hannah dropped the potato and moved closer to him, delving her fingers through his hair, softer to the touch than the eye would lead her to believe and gently massaged the back of his neck. His breathing became rapid. "Do you have any questions so far?"

He shook his head.

Hannah dropped her hand and stepped back. "But the most important part of this particular recipe is the garlic. Garlic is essential to the mechanics of the process. It has unique qualities unlike any other in this world. A wise chef understands garlic, protects it, reveres it and gives it respect. Are you following me so far?"

He nodded.

"First you peel off the delicate protective skin. It's very important to remember the peeling process has to be done painstakingly slowly and very carefully, because you don't want to hurt the tender, supple clove underneath."

"I never knew about peeling it slowly. I always put the garlic, skin and all, on the counter, and bang it with a coffee mug until all the cloves are crushed."

"Sometimes it's nice to do that, you know, if you need a quick bang." Hannah nodded. "But, believe me when I tell you anything worth doing, Chance, is worth doing slowly. You have to savor each sensation." She placed her hand around his neck again and leaned close to his ear, drawing her body nearer.

She said very softly, her voice husky with longing, "Then you take that plump piece of garlic...it should be plump by the way, that's very important, and you place it in the palm of your hand."

She moved even closer into him, cradling her hips into his hardness. "You have to use your muscles to press and release, press and release—"

He groaned.

She pressed.

"Until you've extracted every last bit of juice out. That piece of garlic has to be squeezed just so." She showed him her fist, which she pulsated several times before placing it back on his neck. "You do that until it has nothing left to give."

Chance's brown-eyed gaze traveled down her face, neck, shoulders. With the soft pad of his finger, he lightly skimmed the top of her breasts, which were exposed to his view over the bib apron.

Hannah took a deep, shuddering breath. "Finally, you ooze some ketchup inside a glass. You fill the rest of the glass with liquid, making sure the ketchup is completely covered."

His breathing sounded ragged. "With what?"

"Water's okay."

"Water?" He sounded as if he could use some.

"Then you take your utensil, plunge it inside and stir until it's the texture that you like. I prefer stiff. But that's personal, of course. You may like a different texture, more moist, soft." She knew making pot roast tonight was fate.

Chance drew his finger along the contour of her breast, circling her nipple through the apron until it formed a hard peak. "Why are you doing this, Hannah?" he asked softly.

"Why am I doing what?" Her stomach muscles quivered.

"You know, exactly."

"Maybe I think you're a very nice, hungry man," she whispered.

"I'm not nice." He dipped his head and his lips nuzzled the side of her neck. "But I'm very hungry."

She sighed, lost in the pleasure his mouth and tongue provoked. She knew deep down inside her, everything that happened between them from this moment forward would hinge on the next few minutes. "If you're worried about me, you shouldn't be. I know what I'm doing."

He groaned when she placed her hands on his firm buttocks and brought him closer to her, feeling the hardness of him, wanting to ease the yearning inside her, knowing only Chance could do so.

Chance liked the variety of aprons she wore. Tonight's was starched, and so provocative he'd had a hard-on from the moment he walked through her front door.

But he had control over hard-ons. When she reached out and placed both hands on his behind and pulled him to her, nestling him just where he wanted to be, he had to gather all the willpower he could muster, and then some, to keep from laying her down on the kitchen floor and making love to her then and there. He forced himself not to think about the way her fingers gently kneaded his muscles or the way her vanilla scent engulfed him.

Her fingers glided over his chest, his ribs, his stomach and lower, until she reached the hard, swollen part of him, engulfed him with her hand and stopped. "I've been thinking about this all afternoon," she said.

"You have?" His voice came out sounding strangled.

"Oh, yes." Hannah sighed, squeezing him gently. "I think about how garlic and my Heavenly Haven pot roast seem to go together perfectly. Press, release, press, release." Her hand did the motions her voice suggested.

"You don't know what you're doing." His heart raced.

"I know exactly what I'm doing."

Hannah took her hand off his hard sex and Chance breathed again. She gathered both ends of his shirt and pulled him toward her.

He had to stop her before this got out of hand. "Don't stop."

"I wouldn't think of it."

"That's what I'm afraid of," he sighed, willing to go down in defeat.

"Kiss me." Her lips invited, her eyes captivated.

His gaze flickered over her crimson curls, heavily lidded topaz eyes fringed with dark lashes and finally lingered on her moist, pouty lips. He brought his mouth closer, touching softly, gently, outlining their shape with his tongue. Then she parted hers, giving him entrance, inviting him to taste a small piece of the real heaven.

His hands floated down her back and stopped momentarily by the apron's bow. Every muscle in his body was tense, every nerve on fire, and his erection throbbed painfully within the tight restraints of his jeans.

With one pull the bow untied and the apron split open. A gentleness he hadn't known he possessed overcame him. He broke their kiss long enough to lift the apron over her head and throw it on the floor. He unbuttoned the first button on her blouse. She didn't move to stop him. He trailed his finger along the soft, white skin now exposed to his eyes and heard her inhale sharply. He undid the next button, exposing more plump cleavage, and nuzzled each new area of fragrant skin revealed to his gaze. Hannah had her head tilted back, her eyes closed.

Finally, the last button came undone and Chance slipped the shirt off her shoulders and down her arms, exposing a low-cut, wispy white bra that revealed, more than concealed, the delights they protected. His fingers trembled. He felt as if he were a pirate who had finally discovered the ultimate, elusive treasure he had spent a lifetime searching for. Now Hannah watched him, not taking her eyes from his face, a Mona Lisa smile on her lips. He unsnapped the front clasp and drew a quick intake of breath. Her breasts firm and soft, rounded and bountiful, filled his hands. He said reverently, "Even if I denied how much I want you right now, at this very moment, my body would prove me a liar."

"I want you, too." Her voice whispered over him.

"You know I'm leaving town as soon as my job here is over. That no matter how good it is between us, I'm not staying. You're the kind of girl a man marries, has kids with, gets a dog with." As he stroked the dusky tips and felt them peak under his fingers, his body became even more tightly strung, begging its own release. His voice raspy with need, he said, "Commitment isn't part of the deal."

"You've told me that before."

"There's no future between us, Hannah. When we do this, you and I together, it would only be for sex. Only sex. Just for the immediate pleasure two bodies have when they come together for release."

Only sex? Did he really believe that what was happening between them was a onetime immediate slam-bam-thank-you-ma'am kind of relationship? Hannah stared into his eyes. His mouth had been set in a firm, grim line, yet his eyes looked back at her with warmth. And tenderness. And undeniable hunger.

His eyes told the truth, his lips spread the lie. Those chocolate-brown orbs were the window into his deepest thoughts and dreams. His very soul. Poor Chance. So very misguided about his own future with her. She had no choice but to help him take the right path toward happiness.

When she gave herself to Chance, it would be for a lifetime commitment and nothing less. And for him, she could sacrifice tonight's promise of pleasure in order to bring both of them a future of happiness and love. She deserved the best. Him.

Chance needed her to help him recognize the feelings he fought so hard against. She knew he loved her, too, or why else had he insisted on giving her driving lessons, when her driving was perfect? Why had he forgiven her so easily, when his car had been damaged not once but twice? Why did he seek her out when he wasn't working, like the day he had come to the Fritz-Simmonses' house under the guise of helping with the tea party? For one reason only. He had fallen in love with her and had to be near her—because when people are in love, they can barely stand being apart.

And on top of all that, not only had he spoken the words *commitment* and *children* in the same sentence, he added the one word, the magic word, that told her all she needed to know about how he really felt. *Dogs.* No man mentioned getting a dog unless he was truly ready to settle down with one woman.

And she, Hannah Hart, knew exactly how to help Chance realize what he felt for her was love and not lust. He was a man, wasn't he? And didn't all men crave what they couldn't have until they went crazy with wanting? She knew, theoretically, denying him what they both wanted, very desperately, would help him conclude that if they had a future together as one, he would never be denied her again. Just as she had predicted from almost the moment she had met him, it all came down to the very simple, age-old theory of leading a thirsty dog to water, then making him beg. She'd have Chance begging for commitment within a week.

"You know what?" Hannah stepped away from him in order to break the strong electrical surges running between them. She resnapped the bra clasp, picked up her blouse from the floor, slipped it on, then gushed, "You're right! You have me pegged. I want something more. I deserve something more."

Hannah sat down in a chair on the other side of the table, smiled sweetly and said, "I haven't had a lot of time to think about what almost happened here tonight. But it didn't happen, and it has nothing to do with your temporary citizenship or that you're a love 'em and leave 'em kind of guy. It's something else entirely. Something deeper, and more meaningful. Something which, I know when I tell you, will hurt you deeply. I'm not sure I should share this with you."

"It's the commitment thing." He nodded, a smug smile on his lips. "I knew it all the time."

"Commitment?" She laughed. "Oh, no, nothing like that. I wish it were that simple. I mean, you're good-looking, you're a nice guy, and you'd be okay for a good time, but you're not anyone I'd want to settle down with."

His mouth dropped open. Then snapped shut. "Excuse me?"

"I don't want you to think I didn't have fun tonight, as far as it went." She patted her unruly curls. "But you see, Chance, I mean, this is the nineties. And you're just fine for a friend, but, well," she daintily shrugged, "you know how it is."

"No, I don't. Explain it to me."

"Well, it's the sex thing."

"We didn't have sex." He'd known all along it would come to this, he thought smugly. She wasn't a woman of the nineties. She was a throwback from the fifties. Commitment. Children. Dogs. All four-letter words.

"I know. And we won't. I mean, well, I deserve so much more."

"More than me?" He came around to her side of the table, pulled out a chair and sat down, making sure his knees and her knees touched and rubbed a bit.

"Well, yes. Kissing you was nice," she said. "I admit I got kind of excited there for a while. In fact, now that I think about it, it was nice kissing you at the movie theater, too. On a scale of one to ten with ten being high, I'd say your kisses are about a six.''

''Six?'' He clenched his teeth.

''Six is good. You know, it's not a ten, but it's not a five either, which is average. You're slightly above average. You need a little work with some of your tongue movements, but I'm not sure I'm the one to teach you how to reach your full potential.'' She leaned over and patted the top of his knee. ''I'm just too busy right now to take on a charity kiss case.''

He stared at her for a long moment. Then he smirked. ''You're putting me on.''

''No.''

''Yes you are, babe. No one, and I mean no one has ever told me I was less than perfect. Women beg for more. Beg.''

She raised an eyebrow. ''I suppose some women are more easily satisfied than others. You were good as far as it went. But you're not all that great. And I'm predicting, if tonight had gone any further, you'd think it was better than what it really was, because I know on a scale of one to ten, I'm at least an eleven or a twelve. Then you'd want something more permanent, so that you can keep getting all of my good loving and kissing. Meanwhile, I'd only be getting a six.''

Chance didn't know whether to laugh or be angry. He was unratable. Women came after him panting. Hannah was a fruitcake.

But, damn, he wanted to kiss her again. Something fierce.

He stood abruptly; the chair fell backward on the floor. Hannah's head shot up. He pinned her with his most daunting stare. A moment passed, then she gasped and he knew she knew exactly what his thoughts were. He took her by both elbows and drew her out of the chair, flush with every hard part of him. Her breasts pillowed against his chest, her softness cupped the erection that wouldn't die. He put one arm around her waist, the other under her bottom and pulled her as close to him as he could with their clothes still on, lowered his mouth to her already parted lips and greedily explored the sweet, moist recesses. Not until he felt her shudder and heard her moan, did he drop his arms and step back.

Chance scanned Hannah's flushed cheeks and glazed eyes. He took in the rapid rise and fall of those incredible, now regretfully covered breasts and listened to her breaths coming out in short, shallow bursts.

He moved toward the kitchen door, glanced at the clock above the stove, then yanked the door open. He had to meet Chief Turley at the school across from the concession stand in ten minutes and had lost track of time. With one last look at Hannah standing prone by the table, he brought his hand to his forehead and saluted her before walking out the door. "See you around, babe."

"BABE?" WAS THAT the endearment of a man whose bachelorhood was about to be history? She listened as he took the steps two at a time, heard the Mustang's door open and shut, the motor start and the car back out of the driveway.

There was a frustrating fire raging inside her and the only thing she knew to do about it was get her mind off of Chance and the lovemaking that hadn't happened, and to go to work. She grabbed her keys, got in the Tank and headed for the concession stand. She didn't think Elvin would mind if she borrowed some sugar to build a scaled-down model of the Sugar Land city hall for the kids, so they would have a guide when they created their own model at the fair.

On the drive over to the park, she did her best to convince herself that she'd done the right thing tonight, sending Chance away. She knew, though, if she ever had the opportunity to repeat the whole evening, she might not be strong enough to make the same decision again.

CHANCE DROVE THE windshieldless Mustang slowly past District Park Number Six. The concession stand was lit up like a Christmas tree. Two white trucks, similar to the one Henry Perkins, Mac's murdered campaign manager, had been found in, a Mercedes and a Buick were parked in the lot. "Bingo." He blew out a long-held breath of air.

Across the street from the concession stand was a school, and Chance turned into the driveway and parked in the lot behind the building. Chief Turley and twelve officers were waiting for him in unmarked vehicles.

"Did you have time to set up the hidden cameras?" Chance asked as he adjusted his gun in the waistband of his jeans and fixed his long shirttails to camouflage the weapon.

"There's one in the storage room and another by the door," Turley answered.

Chance nodded. Minutes later, he stood in the doorway of the concession stand. Elvin held the clipboard and counted boxes. Mac followed along with a red marker, placing a line over the inventoried cartons.

Chance cleared his throat and both men looked up. "Mac." He acknowledged the short, balding man who glared at him though wire-rimmed glasses. "Elvin, kind of expected to see you here tonight." Chance walked through the door, his head buzzing, blood racing through his veins.

Elvin's face had turned pale under his winter tan. Chance picked up a box of sugar. When his instincts worked they really worked. His blood practically boiled over. He held the box out to Elvin. "Open this."

"I don't think that's necessary," Elvin said.

"For some reason, I do." Chance ripped the lid and white powder blew in the air. Then, like a dust cloud, it settled on the floor. "What a mess." He sounded contrite. "That doesn't look like any sugar I've ever seen. Wonder what it could be?"

Elvin lunged for him as Mac tried to back out the door. Pushing Elvin aside, Chance, adrenaline pumping, went after Mac, stopping him before he could leave the building. "I'm a cop, you piece of crap." He grabbed Mac by the shirt collar, dragged him across the floor and shoved his back against the wall. "And you're under arrest."

Mac's body jerked forward, trying to escape from Chance's death grip, while a stream of obscenities spewed from his mouth. Chance pushed him into the wall again, holding him there with a knee shoved into his rib cage.

Suddenly, every ounce of fire burning through his veins, every part of his being that defined what he did for a living, all those hunches he depended on for his survival, vanished. Hannah walked up to the building.

She stopped in the doorway, looked around, a slight smile on her lips. "Hi, everyone. Didn't expect to see anybody here this late. What's going on? Chance, what are you doing to Mac? I don't like him much, either, but isn't that a little harsh?"

Chance had to get her out of there. These men were killers and she had just placed both their lives on the line. "Leave," he ordered.

Hannah's smile faltered. "That's not very friendly."

"Now."

"I'm not leaving without at least three cartons of this sugar," she said stubbornly.

"Yes, you are."

"No, I'm not. Elvin, I brought my dolly. If you could put three, no make that four cartons in my car, I'd be so grateful."

Elvin backed himself toward the counter where the soda machines were, opened the drawer and pulled out a silver gun. His gaze flickered over Chance, Mac and Hannah. He pointed it at Chance and said, "Let go of him or you're dead."

Hannah, her hands on her hips, gasped. "What are you doing? Is that thing real? Oh, God, put that away. I'm sure when tonight's over and I reflect back on this evening, I'll really appreciate what's going on here, as soon as I figure it all out. But right now, let's all put away our anger and realize that's it's only sugar."

"Shut up, little Miss Sunshine," Mac hissed, not taking his eyes off of Chance. "Do what Elvin says, or he'll kill your friend."

Chance dropped his hand and moved away from Mac.

Hannah came undone. She flew at Elvin, slapping at his arms. "Put that thing down, right now. Right now, do you hear me?"

Elvin's hand shook. "Be quiet, Hannah. Please, I have to think."

"You don't have any brains to think with. I can't believe this. You know, I was against Texas passing that concealed-weapons law, and this is exactly why."

She ran toward Chance, pushing her back and bottom into his stomach and zipper. He knew he should be thinking about getting her out of there, and yet all he could focus on was how good she felt against him.

"Elvin, I'm going to write my congressman. You're act-

ing absolutely unstable,'' Hannah chewed him out, her
arms flung wide, her body a shield.

"Move away from him, let me get a clean shot.'' Elvin
waved the weapon.

"I will not. That thing may go off.''

"Hannah—'' Chance tried to push her aside, but she
wouldn't budge. "Do as he says,'' Chance coaxed.
"Please. I won't let anything happen to you or me.''

"If Elvin wants to shoot you, he's going to have to go
through me to do it. Mac, though, forget it. I'm not risking
my life to save him.''

"You don't realize how dangerous they are,'' he whispered into her ear.

"All I wanted was some sugar. A simple yes or no
would have been fine.''

"It's heroin,'' Elvin yelled.

Mac lunged toward Elvin. "You're dead. You're all
dead.'' He grabbed the gun out of Elvin's hand, waving it
at Hannah and Chance. "Get back all of you. Against the
wall. You, too, Elvin, you idiot.''

"Heroin? I don't think so. Is this male testosterone running rampant?'' Hannah's face had turned as red as her
hair, and her body practically hummed in anger.

Chance swung her around to the wall, putting his hand
over her mouth, wanting her to keep quiet long enough so
he could have a chance to get Mac down on the concrete
before she made that piece of vermin so angry he started
shooting.

"I'm going to kill you last, Hannah,'' the snake hissed.
"I want you to see your friends die first and to know it's
all your fault. You never did bring out the best in me.
You've always gotten in the way. The only reason Ada
gets elected mayor is because everyone loves her daughter.'' His voice was nasty. "Now here you are again, ev-

eryone's darling, ready to ruin my million-dollar operation. Your time on earth is over. Your luck just ran out.''

She looked at Chance. ''Have you seen your life flash before your eyes?''

He shook his head.

''Me, either.''

Chance relaxed his hold and she shrugged out of his grasp, moving away from his reach. She stood in front of Mac, pushed the arm that held the gun and said, ''Give that to me, right now.''

''Don't you get it? Are you that stupid? This heroin is leaving tonight and when it goes, you'll be going, too. You clowns aren't going to get in the way.''

Hannah let out a bloodcurdling yell, swung her hand under his gun-toting arm and kicked Mac in the groin. He dropped the gun and doubled over, whimpering.

''You were always such a loser.'' She dusted her hands.

''Get down on your belly.'' Chance came behind her brandishing a bigger gun, pointing first at Mac, then Elvin.

Mac slowly went down and Chance held him in place, digging a foot in the small of his back, pointing the gun at Elvin's head.

''Is that your gun or mine?'' Elvin stuttered.

''If you can't tell the difference between a .22 and a .357, you shouldn't be carrying one.''

Elvin shrunk against the wall. ''Well, mine wasn't loaded.''

Mac, his face smashed into the concrete, swore. Hannah rolled her eyes. ''I can't believe this. Chance, why do you have a gun?''

''I'm a cop.''

''A what?''

''We'll talk later.''

''I want to talk now. How come you kept this a secret?

Why is everyone leading a double life? Elvin's dealing in heroin, you're a cop. And I'm Cinderella. Great. The only person who's exactly who I always thought he was is Mac, and he's pond scum."

Hannah turned on her heels, disgusted with the lot of them, and left the concession stand. She passed Chief Turley and his herd of officers on her way back to the Tank. If Chance being a cop was a big secret, and he was only pretending to be a parks director, then he must have been brought here for one reason. To find what he had found. Heroin. And that could only mean one thing. He was only here temporarily, as he had been telling her all along. When his job was over he'd be leaving.

11
_____

SEVERAL DAYS HAD PASSED and Hannah still hadn't talked to Chance about what had happened at the concession stand. She needed him to answer her thousands of questions. But Ed, the traitor, had betrayed her. He'd loaned Chance his purple Chevy to use until the Mustang's windshield could be replaced, giving him the freedom to keep away from the house.

Oh, sure, Hannah had seen him briefly during those days. The first time, she'd said a simple, "I need to talk to you." He smiled, gave her shoulder a friendly squeeze.

"Have to get to the police station. We'll talk later," he'd said.

The next time she said, "Please, I have to ask you about that night." And again he walked away with the promise of talking "later." Only later never came.

Once she happened upon him by accident, as she puttered by the shrubs near the driveway. She had waited hours for an accidental meeting. She had worn the most enticing outfit she owned, a blue-jean skirt that barely covered her bottom, and sometimes didn't, and a red knit sweater with a neckline down to her navel, black fishnet stockings and a red garter belt. What man could possibly walk away from that? Chance did. He barely glanced at her.

Now she knew the sleepless nights, the walk-around-like-a-zombie days, her short temper, the way she burst into tears over the slightest provocation, were all Chance's fault.

If that wasn't enough, her normally positive, uplifting disposition had taken a 180-degree turn in the opposite direction, which caused everything that could go wrong in her life to happen. Her cookies burned. Her roses died. Her Tank had a flat. Her mother called, not once but four or five times a day.

All Hannah wanted was five minutes so she could ask Chance, straight out, if he was staying or leaving. And he wouldn't give her the time. Her days and nights had been tortured with the knowledge that fate had taken an ugly turn.

The night before the Faire, she had finally fallen into a deep, depressed, exhausted sleep. When she awoke the next morning, the one morning in her life when the kids were depending on her and she couldn't be late—she was late. And that was Chance's fault, too, because she had unintentionally fallen asleep on the living-room couch. The alarm clock was in the bedroom.

With barely twenty minutes to take a shower, get dressed and drive to the concession stand, she had to rush. And that was Chance's fault, too. Because everyone in the whole world knew when Hannah had to rush, something bad happened. Like the time she backed into his Mustang.

When she left the house the first time, she forgot her keys. The second time she was halfway down the block when she remembered she hadn't taken her insulin. She drove back, ran inside the house and grabbed her back-pack, throwing the insulin kit inside and mentally reminding herself to take the shot as soon as she got to the park. Then she grabbed some cheese and bread, stuffed food down her throat and headed back out the door for the third time, when she collided with the elusive Mr. Secret Agent Man McCoy.

"What are you doing here?" she asked, hurrying down the steps.

"It's time we talked." He followed.

She looked back at him. Those dark, sexy eyes were filled with hunger—and perhaps regret. "Isn't it convenient for you to want to talk at this very moment, when you know I was supposed to have been at the concession stand ten minutes ago. Or did you forget about the Faire?"

"No, I'm going to help, just like I promised." He kept up with her rapid pace until they reached the Tank.

She threw open the car door and tossed her backpack on the seat, then handed him the keys. "Get in. But remember this. I'm only letting you drive because I want to concentrate on all the things I've been saving up to say to you for the past couple of days, and I don't want any kind of distraction to come in the way."

Hannah used the first five minutes to put all the feelings that had been simmering inside in some kind of order. Finally, very slowly, very clearly, she spelled it out for him. "You know by now I'm not a morning person, so normally I wouldn't be able to think this clearly so early, but I've had a couple of days to ponder the whole episode."

"I owe you an explanation and an apology."

"Yes, you do. But you don't have to apologize for being a secret agent. It's not your fault that you're not in the same league as James Bond. You're more like Inspector Clouseau of the Pink Panther movies. But even he was able to get the job done. Granted it was in a bumbling, odd sort of way, but that's okay." She patted his knee in sympathy. "Not everyone can be James Bond. You shouldn't feel bad about that."

Chance glanced at her, his expression grim. "In that

quirky brain of yours, you've hit the problem right on the head. Before I met you, I was James Bond. For some reason though, whenever I'm near you, I become Jacques Clouseau.''

"It's the karate chop I gave to Mac, isn't it? Your male ego suffered.''

"You're half-right.''

"I knew it.'' She slapped her hand on his knee and the car jerked forward. "I'm going to tell you something right now. I don't play the femme fatale for any man. If there's trouble, I'm going to fix it to the best of my abilities.''

"It's not that at all, Hannah.'' Chance pulled into the parking lot at the concession stand and turned to face her. "Listen, we'll talk after the Faire. You've got a mass of little hellions waiting for you over there. I hope you've got an alternative plan for building that model.'' He handed her the car keys.

"I always have an alternative plan.''

Hannah hurried to the children. She unlocked the concession stand door, then turned to the waiting crowd. Her palms had begun to sweat and she wiped them on the back of her shorts, then blotted the sheen of perspiration off her forehead with a tissue. "Okay, kids, we have some important issues to discuss, so listen up.''

She looked over her team of Angels. All bright eyed and innocent. Even Peter had come. "By now, you all know what happened here the other night.'' She waited until the murmurs of agreement died down. "We've had to modify our plans. Instead of sugar boxes, we're going to use candy boxes. This will work out even better since there will be a more varied quantity of shapes and colors—making the replica of city hall come out even better. How's that sound to everyone?''

All the kids cheered. Hannah had a feeling they would.

Chance helped pass out the boxes, and as each child left the Faire, she warned, "Don't eat the candy!"

Royal Sugar Company had closed off Sweet Sugar Boulevard to traffic and the twentieth annual Sugar Land Faire and minicarnival took place on the street where Sugar Land had gotten its name.

The Faire didn't officially begin until eleven, giving the teams in the league three hours to build their exhibits.

While Hannah loved her Angels to death, they were purposely doing things to distract her, so they could sneak candy. The little devils tore up the empty boxes and threw the evidence away, instead of using the boxes to build walls. Suddenly she was running out of candy boxes, city hall was lopsided and she was feeling pretty loopy herself.

"Hannah, over here." LaVerne waved boxes of Mars bars in the air. "I have to show you this. It's important."

"Hannah, I need you a minute!" Wendy called out from the other side of the booth. "It's tipping."

"Coach Hannah, Peter is eating the licorice candy," Trish tattled.

"Am not, Coach Hannah," Peter denied, grinning through black teeth.

"Morning, Hannah." Chief Turley came up behind her, pointing to the model. "Interesting thing you've put together there."

"Thanks." Hannah turned and her head reeled. She put her fingers to her temples, trying to steady herself.

"About the other night—"

"Don't say a word about it. I happened to walk in at the wrong place at the right time." Her hand began to shake. "Or maybe the right place at the wrong time. Or the right place at the right time. I don't know." She wasn't feeling good, at all.

Vicki tugged at Hannah's shirt and looked up at her, a

pained expression on her face. "Coach Hannah, I gotta go to the bathroom. It's gonna leak out."

Hannah put an arm around Vicki's small shoulders, as much to steady herself as to comfort the child. "Bathroom. Yes."

She found Chance talking to a police officer who'd come dressed as a clown. "I'm taking Vicki to the rest room. Would you please watch the booth and make sure the kids don't eat any more of the display?"

He nodded, and shouted out, "Don't eat the candy."

The children glanced over in his direction and continued to stuff boxes down their shirts.

Hannah kneeled down, feeling under the booth for her backpack. A wave of dizziness overcame her when she straightened back up again. More sweat broke out on her forehead, and her hands had become cold and clammy. She closed her eyes for a moment to clear her vision before taking Vicki by the hand and walking quickly toward the rest rooms in Royal Sugar's tourist office.

Mothers called out to her, asking questions, friends tried to delay her, begging a moment of time, but Hannah, with Vicki in tow, stopped for no one.

Vicki went in one stall and Hannah in another. Leaning against the closed door, she dropped the backpack on the floor and opened the zipper pocket, taking out her insulin kit. With shaking hands she rubbed the alcohol swab on her thigh and threw the cotton in the commode. She could hardly hold the syringe still enough to insert it through the rubber top of the first bottle, and it took several stabs before she got it in the second, withdrawing more than the normal dose to make up for what she had missed that morning.

Pinching her thigh together, she stuck the needle in, working by feel since she could barely see. She removed the needle, opened the stall door and staggered out, holding her arms out toward where the sink had been. She reached for the rim, missed and crumpled to the cold tile floor.

"Coach!" Vicki screamed as she ran out of the stall, the door banging against the wall. She dropped to her knees by Hannah's side.

"Get Chance."

"Coach," Vicki sobbed burying her head in Hannah's belly. "Don't die."

Hannah didn't think she was going to die, but if she was, she wanted to tell Chance she thought he was special. That she loved him. That she didn't blame him, really and truly, in her heart, for making her rush around this morning, causing her to delay taking her insulin. She couldn't die until he knew that when she did die, it wouldn't be his fault. "Please. Go find Chance."

CHANCE SAW VICKI running like a tornado right to him. He barely had time to brace himself when she knocked into him, flinging her arms around his waist. Her small body, racked by sobs, shook uncontrollably. "Coach, Hannah's dying. I killed her. She took her shot, saw me in the mirror and fell over, dying."

Ada hurried over to Chance and Vicki. All the activity around the booth had stopped. The team looked at him, distress on every single face. He unclipped the cellular phone from his belt and handed it to Ada, ordering, "Call 911. Now. Hannah's in trouble." He grabbed a half-eaten chocolate bar from Chucky's hand and ran.

Chance found Hannah on the floor, her hands clenched on top of her stomach, one leg straight out, the other bent at the knee. He placed his head near her heart. "No, Hannah,'' he moaned, hearing the faint heartbeat. "Please, God, no.''

He sat on the floor, taking her head in his lap. Then, he broke off a small piece of chocolate and slipped it between her lips. "Come on, sweetheart. Chew it down." She didn't respond.

"Hannah." He gathered her in his arms. "The ambulance should be here any minute. I hear the sirens."

Her eyelids fluttered.

"Don't leave me," he begged, holding her near his heart, willing his strength to enter into her. "I love you."

Her breathing weakened.

"Is this what happens when I confess my love? You go into shock and die on me? Well, I refuse to let you. Do you hear me? I love your baking." He rocked her gently back and forth. "I love your driving." He stroked her soft curls. "You can't leave me when my ranking's so low." He lowered his head and murmured close to her ear, "Not when I've just found happiness."

Emergency medical technicians stormed the rest room. Lifting a syringe filled with glucose into the air, the woman paramedic smiled, then plunged it inside Hannah. "This one's for you," she said.

"Will she be okay?" Chance had gotten up from the floor and stood to the side, hovering near.

"She'll be fine. Hannah's normally very careful, but sometimes emergencies happen. And we want to keep our Hannah healthy."

A hand touched his arm, and Chance tensed. "Let the paramedics have room," Ada said. "Go outside now. This has happened before. She'll be up and around in no time." When he didn't move, she gently repeated, "Go outside."

He found the adults and children lining the walkway leading to the tourist office, waiting for word on Hannah, refusing to leave until they saw her. When she was finally brought out on a gurney, the crowd formed a parade, following behind until they reached the ambulance. The children cried; the parents looked anxious. After the ambulance left, not one person moved until several minutes after the taillights disappeared from view.

Chance stood alone on the fringes, as he always had, until Ada broke from the crowd and came over to him.

"Thank you for saving her. I'll always be indebted to you for this."

Chance knew how hard it must have been for her to say that. She didn't want to owe a Yankee.

"You don't owe me, Ada. Helping Hannah seems to be a group project in this town."

"Perhaps. I'd better get to the hospital. I don't want her to be alone too long."

LATE THAT AFTERNOON, Chance paced up and down Hannah's living room staring at the woman sitting on her goose-down couch, looking no worse than a strawberry ice-cream sundae without so much as a lick being taken. She'd only been home from the hospital an hour, but instead of acting weak, she wanted to talk. Where did all this strength come from?

"How come you didn't tell me from the beginning that you were some kind of know-it-all secret agent?" Her eyes were wide and curious, her skin clear and smooth.

"It was a secret."

Hannah lowered her lashes, and whispered the words. "Is there any possibility you'll stay here?"

"I've told you, since the first day we met, that I'd be leaving."

"Yes, you did."

"Hannah—"

"You also told me that you loved me."

"You heard that?"

She nodded.

"I thought you were dying."

"Does that make a difference?"

"No." Chance sat next to her, taking her hand between both of his, rubbing the palm and knuckles. So soft. So gentle. "Remember what I told you about my sister?"

She nodded.

"When Dad died, my mother worked two jobs to support us. Nina started running around with a bad bunch of kids, skipping school, doing weird things. My mom didn't know, but I did. And I ignored it. When Nina overdosed, I blamed myself. I should have stopped her."

"Nina made her choices, and you can't take responsibility for the bad ones."

"Listen to me." He bolted from the couch and paced. "I have this sixth sense. It's inside me. Hunches. I know when things are going to happen. I knew something was wrong with my sister, but I was too busy with work, school and basketball. I shut her problems out."

Hannah's eyes were filled with understanding and compassion—and pain.

"My boss called two days ago. My Cancún vacation's canceled again." He snorted. "I'm needed back in D.C., to take care of another problem that only my sixth sense can figure out. If it still works."

"Are you going?" She looked down at her fingers, folded in her lap.

"I can't stay here. My whole adult life, my reason for existing is because I help communities remove the elements that plague society. I don't know how to do anything else."

"That's very noble."

"I thought so, too, until now. Something happens to me around you. I had a hint of it the first day of practice. I had been to the park twice before and felt danger each time. During practice, I felt nothing. But I didn't put it all together until that night at the concession stand. My fingers were on fire, I knew the heroin was in the sugar boxes, and suddenly, you walked in and I felt nothing. Every instinct in my body disappeared."

"Are you sure you're not thinking of excuses, because you're upset that I gave Mac the old chop-chop and you didn't get to?"

"I'm serious. How can I stay here when you're my weakness? You interfere with my instincts, and yet around you is where I want to be."

"I guess you can't. I saw your Mustang's back. When are you leaving?"

"Soon."

"Would you think me awful if I asked you to make me dinner tonight?" She looked down at her hands, her thumbs, the only sign of inner turmoil, twirled restlessly around each other. "I don't know if I'm strong enough, and if you're leaving, I'd like to share your last meal here."

CHANCE'S KITCHEN WAS so small that when she took a deep breath her breasts brushed his chest. It wasn't enough, it would never be enough. She wanted to close her eyes, reach out, pull him near, feel him all over. But she didn't.

"Dinner's ready." Chance washed lettuce, giving her a view of his backside. Not that it was a bad view, but it just wasn't what she wanted. "Would you get the dressing out of the refrigerator?" he asked.

Hannah looked inside. "I don't see salad dressing."

"There's a bowl of homemade stuff on the second shelf."

"You're a dressing purist."

"No." His voice rumbled. "I'm an undressing purist."

Hannah closed the refrigerator door slowly, letting his words sink in.

"You want to know what I rate myself at undressing?" Chance shut off the water and faced her. "On a scale of one to ten. A thirty."

Hannah's insides began to quake, and her knees started to shake. And this time, it wasn't because she had over-medicated herself. She brushed her tongue along her dry lips. Chance gave her mouth his full attention.

Hannah walked to the dining area. He followed. She sat down, and he took the chair next to hers. Her foot began to tap. He placed his hand on her knee, stilling the move-ment. Warmth radiated where his palm rested, traveling up her legs and pooling inside her belly. Her body went still, her mind raced. "I've been thinking," she said.

"You have?" Strong lips formed a wry grin.

"There's so much to say." She spoke softly, straight-ened her shoulders, thrust her breasts outward, and her hand reached behind her neck as she stretched. Chance's gaze followed her pantherlike movements. She crossed one leg over the other. Her shoe slipped halfway off her foot, dangling from her toes.

His gaze dropped to her foot. Hannah let the shoe drop and his head jerked up. She breathed deeply, uncrossed her leg, lifted her foot until her toes rested on his knee and her tight, straight skirt was hiked higher up her thigh.

"Hannah?" Chance's voice questioned, low, husky. He leaned forward in the chair. Brushing his fingers over her toes, he cupped her heel and kneaded. "You're not talking, Hannah." His deep voice surrounded her, captured her. He circled her ankle, lifting her leg, bringing her foot to his lips.

"This little piggy went to market." He nipped her big toe.

Liquid heat radiated up her leg, pooling into her center.

"This little piggy went home." He moved to the next toe.

"This little piggy had roast beef." His tongue circled her middle toe, then he kissed it.

"And this poor, little piggy had none." Chance's lips gently suckled the next toe.

Hannah's breath caught. The butterflies in her belly fluttered.

"And this little piggy..." He kissed her baby toe and the soft skin underneath. "Ran all the way home begging, kiss me." His lips reached her ankle. "Kiss me." Then her knee. "Kiss me." He continued on to the inside of her thigh, nibbling on the creamy inner skin.

Hannah didn't move. She couldn't. Her leg muscles had turned to Jell-O. Her brain mush. There was a place deep inside her that only Chance could reach. A place coiled tightly, craving release. She shifted restlessly in the chair, holding back the groan of pleasure as his lips traveled farther up her thigh. Fingers massaged her other leg, gliding under her skirt, reaching her silk panties and slipping underneath, finally touching her core.

"Hannah." He moved off the chair, kneeling in front of her, massaging her skin, moving the skirt higher, revealing to his eyes what his fingers had already found.

She arched toward his hand, craving more, the coil in her belly ready to snap.

He taunted her with slow, deliberate strokes, skimming his thumb over her sensitive bud, down the inside of the moist folds of her skin, then up again. She heard the whimper come from deep inside her. She wouldn't go this way alone.

Hannah unsnapped his jeans and painstakingly slowly, torturing him as he had done her, lowered his zipper, releasing his erection from the binding cloth, stroking him until he groaned with the same need.

Chance pulled a condom from his back pocket and ripped open the package with his front teeth.

Hannah took it from him and placed it on the velvet tip of his erection, slowly moving the rubber down the shaft. "Press, release, press, release," she murmured, stroking him.

"I'm having a heart attack here, be kind to me." He took her hands and lifted her to her feet. Sitting back in the chair, he brought her down on top of him, penetrating her, reaching all the way to her heart.

Chance lifted her blouse over her head and threw it on the floor. Her breasts teased him from beneath turquoise lace. He unsnapped the bra, capturing one nipple with his lips and bringing the other to a peak with his fingers, while moving her back and forth on his engorged flesh.

Hannah reached behind her, cupping him, squeezing gently, feeling him expand inside her.

With one swift motion, Chance stood with Hannah's legs wrapped around his waist and laid her gently on top of the quilt, coming home above her. "Have I told you I think you're beautiful?"

She shook her head.

"You are. And kind and sweet, lovely and unique."

"Mr. Shakespeare, be quiet already." She squeezed his shaft with her muscles as tightly as she could. "Don't make me beg."

He kissed her lips gently, teasing her deliberately, making her sorry she'd made fun of his sonnet. Only his torturous plan backfired. She scattered hot, moist kisses on his neck, then met his lips again, consuming him with her tongue. He moved with slow strokes, not taking his mouth from her lips, his tongue echoing the movements of his sex.

Hannah broke the kiss, nuzzling the soft place behind his ear, traveling down the hollow of his neck, licking and suckling him as he moved faster inside her.

The coil began to explode. She wanted to stop it from happening, wanted it to go on forever, but he stroked her harder, quicker, until she shattered, and with one final thrust, he found his own release.

They lay, arms and legs tangled together, until their breathing slowed and the sweat from their bodies dried and chilled. Chance pulled the quilt out from under them, covering them both. He circled her waist and drew her closer to the slow, steady beating of his heart.

"Thank you for tonight," he said softly. "I'm going to miss you, when I go. I wish it didn't have to be this way. I've never felt like this before. Like I've found myself, then lost my way."

She lightly ran her fingers through his hair until his chest rose in the slow, even rhythm of sleep. She wished she had the power to keep him here. But he had a calling stronger than their love.

Hannah gently kissed his cheek and slipped out from the bed. She gathered her scattered clothes and slowly dressed. She opened the door and turned, taking one last look at the man sleeping peacefully on the bed, then closed the door behind her.

12

"SMELLS GOOD IN HERE." Chance entered Hannah's kitchen, with a "morning after a great night" smile on his lips and concern in his eyes. "What could Hannah, the wonder cook, be baking? Doughnuts, right? Yep, that's what it is.

"Only, and I'm guessing here, but I think, instead of frying, you baked them. It's more healthy. And forget flour or your old standby, pancake batter. Too mundane. You'd use cornmeal. Then, to be really healthy, you'd top them off with chocolate frosting made from fructose and brown food coloring."

"Very funny." Hannah wasn't laughing. "They're sugar cookies."

He covered his mouth. "Oh, no," he moaned in mock horror.

She glared at him. "You know, you deserved everything you got. Including that broken tooth. At first, I felt sorry for you. I said to myself, Hannah, this poor man is new in town. His car was wrecked, not that I had all that much to do with it, but unfortunately I couldn't prove the condition it was in when I heard the crash. For all I know, it could have been that way—"

"Hannah, I told you you should've called Elvin about the insurance when the accident happened. Now your agent's in jail, and the state board of insurance is looking into his dealings and it may be years, if ever, before you can collect on the accident.''

She turned on the water faucet and started to scrub the cookie sheets. ''Ed fixed your windshield and did the bodywork and paint job for nothing. People here in Sugar Land take care of each other.''

Chance leaned against the wall, staring at her, all teasing gone. ''You left me last night. I thought you'd be there in the morning. I wanted you with me when I woke up.'' What he really wanted was for her to look at him, so he could read her eyes. Not that it would do any good, since his hunches were of no use when she was near.

''I couldn't spend the night. That would mean commitment. And we're not committed.'' With her hands on her hips, yellow rubber gloves dripping water and suds over her apron and floor, she finally looked at him. ''You're leaving me.''

He touched her shoulder. She shrugged away. Dammit. He'd only done his job. In spite of her help. In spite of her.

Hannah turned off the water, threw the gloves on the counter and walked away. He followed her around the table. She pulled out a chair and sat down. Before he could sit in the other chair, she put her feet on the seat, folded her arms under her breasts and looked up.

Chance gazed into her eyes, then down her neck, lingering on her pushed-up breasts, and finally down the length of her legs. Let him look, she told herself. He would never be lucky enough to have her legs wrapped around his waist again. The fool.

Two fingers stroked her kneecap, skimming down her calf until they reached the ankle. She shivered as electric heat trailed down the path his fingers took, and her muscles must have become weaker, because when he lifted both her legs effortlessly off the chair, one-handed, she knew she ought to put forth some resistance. Only by the time she thought about it, he had already sat down, placing the heels of her feet in direct contact with his zipper and his hard sex underneath.

She tried to move her legs off him. He gently held them down. She couldn't concentrate on all the important things she needed to know, needed to ask, since he purposely distracted her by kneading the sensitive balls of her feet.

He leaned his head back and closed his eyes, using his thumbs to sink deeply into the pressure points of her heels. "I never meant to hurt you." The words sounded as if they came from someone else, a spirit.

"You haven't," she denied. "I really need to get up now. As much as I enjoy sitting here with you, as nice as this conversation has been, I've got work to do."

"What kind of work?"

"The kids will be here for the anticipated victory party in about thirty minutes. I still have to take the cookies outside to the yard, put the punch in the bowls. The table's been set up, but there's a lot of last-minute things."

"You mean after all you've been through in the last twenty-four hours, you're having a party?" What did he care? He wasn't her keeper. He was leaving.

She patted his shoulder and gave him a motherly smile. Dammit, she wasn't his mother.

"I'll be all right. I feel fine, like I could run a hundred laps."

"I don't know—" *Shut up, McCoy,* he told himself. *If you keep blubbering, she'll think you want commitment, and you don't.*

"Don't know what?"

"You swim laps."

"Whatever. You'll be here for the party, won't you?"

"No."

"The kids would like to say goodbye. They grew fond of you."

"I have certain feelings for them, too, but Hannah, I mean, they're kids. You know. Little things." He lowered his hand to his waist to show her how tall they were.

She smiled. "They may be small, but they're certainly powerful."

"Amen to that." They laughed.

Chance took her hands in his. Soft hands. Small, delicate hands. Vanilla, her very special scent, wafted toward him. "Hannah." He let her name roll off his tongue, knowing it would haunt him. She would take up his every waking thought and fill his dreams. He had to get away.

"What?" She gazed at him, all pretense of humor gone.

"When I said I wouldn't be here for the party, I meant I wouldn't be here in Sugar Land. I'm leaving now. I came to say goodbye."

Hannah looked down at their intertwined fingers. She reminded herself that the previous night she'd given the thirsty dog a taste of water, but his thirst hadn't been quenched yet. Because if it had been, he wouldn't be leaving.

Chance said, "Don't think for one moment that I'm like Dave. Your being diabetic has nothing, at all, to do with me having to go. It's my job."

"Oh, I know that." Hannah squeezed his hand reassuringly. "I just make bad choices in men. Diabetes doesn't give someone common sense, more's the pity."

"You think I'm a bad choice."

"Oh, no, Chance. Never you." Hold that water over his head, she told herself. Make him beg. "You were my one perfect choice. I'll always think back on the days I shared with you with fond memories. I'll even tell my children about you."

"Your children?" Not that he wanted kids. No way. But he sure as hell didn't want her having kids with someone else. If she was going to have kids, it would have to be with him, and since he was leaving, there was no way she'd have any kids.

"Of course, my children, silly." Hannah's cheeks flushed and her topaz eyes sparkled. "And the next man won't be some secret agent, either. I'll make sure of that."

"Do you have any ideas?"

"About what?"

"Who the next man's going to be? Not that I care, but you know, I'll always have a soft spot for you." He rubbed her hand harder.

"I'll always have a special place in my heart for you, too. And yes, I have a few men picked out. I'll have the chief run them through his computer. This time I'm going to make anyone with serious potential fill out an application."

He didn't like that Cheshire cat smile. She was already thinking of his replacement and he hadn't even left yet. This sucked, big time.

He rubbed her hand harder. She smiled and sighed deeper. "Do you want to come with me to D.C. for a few days?" He couldn't believe he had asked her that. He never invited a woman to come to his home.

"I don't think so."

"I'm serious, Hannah." How dare she say no?

She opened one eye. "I don't think spending any more quality time together is a good idea. So go on to Washington, and have a great life. I understand your needs completely."

"I can't stay here."

"I know. When you're around me, you lose your sixth sense."

"If I stay near you, the danger might kill me."

"Sugar Land is such a deadly place." She sighed contentedly. Suddenly, Hannah pulled her hands out of his grasp and took her feet off his lap. "Chance." She looked directly into his eyes. "I've been accused of many things, but never of killing anyone. I mean, Dave was trying to get his pants down on a ski lift to do the wild thing with his secretary when he fell off and died. I had nothing to do with that. And I would never think of keeping you here. You're a man of the world, and I'm just a small-town girl. Sure I may be brilliant, I may be talented, I may have a 160 IQ, but that doesn't make me the kind of person a man like you would want to tie yourself down with—"

"Right." What did she mean by not wanting to keep him here? He was the one who *had* to go. It wasn't as if he *wanted* to go. He *had* to. It was a matter of life or death. His. "I want you to know," he said sincerely, "that if I ever thought I could make a commitment, it would be to you."

"Well, that's nice. But I don't know if I'd commit myself to you. I mean you were fun, and everything. But you were still only a seven and a half."

"Hannah, you don't mean that," Chance said softly.

"I don't?"

"No, you don't."

"You're right. I don't. See, you saw right through me the whole time. Listen. I hear the kids coming. Can you help me get these trays outside, and then give me a quick peck on the cheek? Maybe you could write me a letter, if you have time? Better yet, let's E-mail."

"E-mail?"

"Sure. Electronic mail, through the computer. It's the nineties thing to do."

He didn't need her to tell him about E-mail. He could have invented E-mail. She was giving up without a fight. Where was her spunk? Wasn't he worth fighting for? Oh, hell, who did she think she was, anyway? Just some woman in a small town, who didn't mean a thing to him in the scheme of his life.

So why was his stomach tied in knots?

He helped her carry the trays to the yard. By the time they had arranged the food, the yard overflowed with little Angels, who acted like anything but, and parents who pretended the kids weren't there.

The mothers had brought cookies and cakes, too. "We didn't think you'd be up to baking, Hannah," they told her.

Even Ada had come along with Chief Turley. Uniformed police officers arrived, and so did Freddy and the Fritz-Simmons sisters. Ada came over and handed Chance a plastic glass filled with punch. "I guess you did a good job. For a Yank," she admitted.

Chance eyed the mayor warily, then pulled her into a hug. "And you're not bad, either, for a politician."

Hannah blew her baseball whistle, and the crowd quieted. "You all know Chance McCoy is our hero of the hour. Can you all believe that he's a policeman in disguise? Like James Bond. Kind of. We should have guessed he wasn't a parks person, since he was one of the worst coaches we ever had. Right, everyone?"

The crowd cheered. Vicki, Trish, Peter and Chucky spat and wiped. Hannah smiled in Chance's direction, an impersonal smile as smiles went. "Chance was going to try and leave before folks got here. He told me he just hates goodbyes."

The crowd vocalized the same sentiment.

"As far as coaching went, for someone who didn't know what he was doing, no one could have done anything better."

"Right!" All the voices, young and old, rose up and yelled, "Speech, speech."

Chance never did like to make speeches, especially unprepared. But he did the best he could under the circumstances. "Thanks. I enjoyed my time here. Remember, kids, keep your noses clean."

"I don't pick my nose," Mike said.

"Yes, you do. I saw you." Jessica argued.

Vicki kicked Mike in the shin. Ah, he'd miss that Vicki.

It took thirty minutes of Texas-style quick goodbyes before he finally made it back to the apartment and could grab his bags. He lingered momentarily by the bed, still unmade and scented with their lovemaking. He brushed his hand over the pillowcase where Hannah's head had rested, picking up two ginger curls left behind and wrapping them carefully in a piece of tissue. Souvenirs, he told himself, slipping the treasure in his wallet, next to her business card.

Chance came down the stairs slowly, looking over the crowd. He dropped the bags next to the Shelby and went back into the yard searching for Hannah.

"Can you move the Tank? You're blocking me." He interrupted her conversation with one of the young officers. A possible replacement?

"Of course. I was just getting Joey's statistics." She smiled too brightly at the man in blue, who now had his chest puffed out. Moving away from Chance and Joey, Hannah called out, "Come on, everyone, line the driveway. Chance is leaving. Let's give him a rousing Sugar

Land send-off." When he caught up to her, she said, "I'm going to get my keys."

Hannah ran up the stairs, hesitating at the top landing, looking down into the yard. The children and adults walked Chance back to his car. He didn't look happy.

"Hannah?" Ada had followed her into the kitchen. "Are you going to be okay?"

"He's leaving, you know," Hannah said softly, sadly. "You were right all along."

"Maybe I was wrong, darling."

"Only about one thing. He wasn't a mistake. He's just a lost soul. I thought I could help him find peace and love. But whatever he's searching for, I wasn't enough to fill the void."

Ada put her arm around Hannah's shoulders and squeezed. "Go kiss him goodbye and then get on with your life. There's a whole future out there waiting for you."

Hannah hugged her mother. "I love you."

She ran down the stairs, across the driveway and over to where Chance stood next to his classic 1965 cherry-red Mustang Shelby. He really did love that car. But sometimes, a girl had to do what a girl had to do. Men could be so stubborn.

"I'd like one more goodbye kiss," she said.

"Thought you'd never ask." He wrapped his arms around her waist and brought her to him, flesh to flesh. He tilted her head back and captured her lips with his own. His tongue slipped inside her mouth, feasting, remembering. Bittersweet and lonely. And she knew, then, knew with all her heart, that no matter what he said, he didn't want to go.

Chance watched Hannah sway to the Tank, her long, beautiful legs poetry in motion. She slid inside and closed the car door, turned the key and gunned the engine. When it was humming along as well as any diesel could hum, she waved at him and put the car in gear.

He turned away and bent down to pick up his bags. The crowd's cheerful racket almost drowned out the sound of the crash. He spun in time to see the Tank making love with his Shelby. Again.

Hannah lay slumped over the steering wheel. Not moving. The crowd became silent. Their eyes were wide in horror. Smoke poured from the engines. Radiators hissed.

Hannah. He loved her. He'd killed her. This was all his fault. He hadn't wanted to leave her. He had wanted to stay, but he'd been too much of a coward to admit he was terrified of starting all over. Of not succeeding. He prayed for one more opportunity to begin his life over again. With her.

Chance yanked the Tank's door open. "Hannah! Hannah talk to me. Please talk to me." He reached inside. "Did you forget to take your insulin? Did you eat this morning?" He ran his hands over her neck, back, arms and legs, feeling for breaks. She moaned. He asked, "Where's it hurt?" He gently prodded her rib cage.

"Am I in heaven?"

"You're not dead."

"You're wrong," Hannah said dreamily. "I'm in heaven with an angel who sounds like Chance but asks questions like my mother."

He chuckled. Hannah. How could he even think of leaving her? Where were his brains last night? She couldn't take care of herself. She needed him. Who was he kidding? He needed her.

"Chance, can you move aside a bit so I can get out?"

"What?"

"I don't have any insurance you know," she said, as

he reached for her arm to help her. "Although I'll deny this is my fault. I had put the Tank in reverse, when I meant drive."

He looked at the dead Shelby. No anger. No regret. Well, maybe a bittersweet twinge. He drew Hannah close to him, feeling at peace for the first time since his father had died. "When I thought you were dead, I felt dead. When you talked about finding my replacement, I went crazy inside. Which reminds me, give me the paper with Joey's statistics."

She handed it over with a smile.

"When I told you I loved you, I didn't know you could hear me, but I meant every word. I do love you. More than life itself."

"I love you, too. In fact, on a scale of one to ten, I love you a fifty."

"Only a fifty?" He raised one eyebrow.

"You're going to have to earn your way up to a hundred, big boy." Hannah winked. "Do you think you can make it?"

He lifted her chin and looked straight into her big eyes. "With you by my side for the rest of my life, I can do anything."

and

HARLEQUIN®

I N T R I G U E ®

Double Dare ya!

Identical twin authors Patricia Ryan and
Pamela Burford bring you a dynamic duo of
books that just happen to feature identical twins.

Meet Emma, the shy one, and her diva double,
Zara. Be prepared for twice the pleasure and
twice the excitement as they give two
unsuspecting men trouble times two!

In April, the scorching **Harlequin Temptation** novel
#631 **Twice the Spice** by Patricia Ryan

In May, the suspenseful **Harlequin Intrigue** novel
#420 **Twice Burned** by Pamela Burford

Pick up both—if you dare....

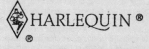

MILLION DOLLAR SWEEPSTAKES
OFFICIAL RULES
NO PURCHASE NECESSARY TO ENTER

1. To enter, follow the directions published. Method of entry may vary. For eligibility, entries must be received no later than March 31, 1998. No liability is assumed for printing errors, lost, late, non-delivered or misdirected entries.

   To determine winners, the sweepstakes numbers assigned to submitted entries will be compared against a list of randomly, preselected prize winning numbers. In the event all prizes are not claimed via the return of prize winning numbers, random drawings will be held from among all other entries received to award unclaimed prizes.

2. Prize winners will be determined no later than June 30, 1998. Selection of winning numbers and random drawings are under the supervision of D. L. Blair, Inc., an independent judging organization whose decisions are final. Limit: one prize to a family or organization. No substitution will be made for any prize, except as offered. Taxes and duties on all prizes are the sole responsibility of winners. Winners will be notified by mail. Odds of winning are determined by the number of eligible entries distributed and received.

3. Sweepstakes open to residents of the U.S. (except Puerto Rico), Canada and Europe who are 18 years of age or older, except employees and immediate family members of Torstar Corp., D. L. Blair, Inc., their affiliates, subsidiaries, and all other agencies, entities, and persons connected with the use, marketing or conduct of this sweepstakes. All applicable laws and regulations apply. Sweepstakes offer void wherever prohibited by law. Any litigation within the province of Quebec respecting the conduct and awarding of a prize in this sweepstakes must be submitted to the Régie des alcools, des courses et des jeux. In order to win a prize, residents of Canada will be required to correctly answer a time-limited arithmetical skill-testing question to be administered by mail.

4. Winners of major prizes (Grand through Fourth) will be obligated to sign and return an Affidavit of Eligibility and Release of Liability within 30 days of notification. In the event of non-compliance within this time period or if a prize is returned as undeliverable, D. L. Blair, Inc. may at its sole discretion, award that prize to an alternate winner. By acceptance of their prize, winners consent to use of their names, photographs or other likeness for purposes of advertising, trade and promotion on behalf of Torstar Corp., its affiliates and subsidiaries, without further compensation unless prohibited by law. Torstar Corp. and D. L. Blair, Inc., their affiliates and subsidiaries are not responsible for errors in printing of sweepstakes and prize winning numbers. In the event a duplication of a prize winning number occurs, a random drawing will be held from among all entries received with that prize winning number to award that prize.

5. This sweepstakes is presented by Torstar Corp., its subsidiaries and affiliates in conjunction with book, merchandise and/or product offerings. The number of prizes to be awarded and their value are as follows: Grand Prize — $1,000,000 (payable at $33,333.33 a year for 30 years); First Prize — $50,000; Second Prize — $10,000; Third Prize — $5,000; 3 Fourth Prizes — $1,000 each; 10 Fifth Prizes — $250 each; 1,000 Sixth Prizes — $10 each. Values of all prizes are in U.S. currency. Prizes in each level will be presented in different creative executions, including various currencies, vehicles, merchandise and travel. Any presentation of a prize level in a currency other than U.S. currency represents an approximate equivalent to the U.S. currency prize for that level, at that time. Prize winners will have the opportunity of selecting any prize offered for that level; however, the actual non U.S. currency equivalent prize if offered and selected, shall be awarded at the exchange rate existing at 3:00 P.M. New York time on March 31, 1998. A travel prize option, if offered and selected by winner, must be completed within 12 months of selection and is subject to: traveling companion(s) completing and returning of a Release of Liability prior to travel; and hotel and flight accommodations availability. For a current list of all prize options offered within prize levels, send a self-addressed, stamped envelope (WA residents need not affix postage) to: MILLION DOLLAR SWEEPSTAKES Prize Options, P.O. Box 4456, Blair, NE 68009-4456, USA.

6. For a list of prize winners (available after July 31, 1998) send a separate, stamped, self-addressed envelope to: MILLION DOLLAR SWEEPSTAKES Winners, P.O. Box 4459, Blair, NE 68009-4459, USA.

Harlequin Romance

celebrates forty fabulous years!

Crack open the champagne and join us in celebrating Harlequin Romance's very special birthday.

Forty years of bringing you the best in romance fiction—and the best just keeps getting better!

Not only are we promising you three months of terrific books, authors and romance, but a chance to win a special hardbound 40th Anniversary collection featuring three of your favorite Harlequin Romance authors. And 150 lucky readers will receive an **autographed** collector's edition. Truly a one-of-a-kind keepsake.

Look in the back pages of any Harlequin Romance title, from April to June for more details.

Come join the party!

LOVE *or* MONEY?
Why not Love *and* Money!
After all, millionaires
need love, too!

How to Marry a
MILLIONAIRE

**Suzanne Forster,
Muriel Jensen
and
Judith Arnold**

bring you three original stories
about finding that one-in-a million man!

Harlequin also brings you
a million-dollar sweepstakes—enter
for your chance to win a fortune!

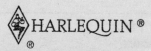 HARLEQUIN ®

HTMM

Free Gift Offer

With a Free Gift proof-of-purchase
from any Harlequin® book, you can receive
a beautiful cubic zirconia pendant.

This stunning marquise-shaped stone is a genuine cubic
zirconia—accented by an 18" gold tone necklace.
(Approximate retail value $19.95)

Send for yours today...
compliments of ✦HARLEQUIN®

To receive your free gift, a cubic zirconia pendant, send us one original proof-of-purchase, photocopies not accepted, from the back of any Harlequin Romance®, Harlequin Presents®, Harlequin Temptation®, Harlequin Superromance®, Harlequin Intrigue®, Harlequin American Romance®, or Harlequin Historicals® title available in February, March or April at your favorite retail outlet, together with the Free Gift Certificate, plus a check or money order for $1.65 U.S./$2.15 CAN. (do not send cash) to cover postage and handling, payable to Harlequin Free Gift Offer. We will send you the specified gift. Allow 6 to 8 weeks for delivery. Offer good until April 30, 1997, or while quantities last. Offer valid in the U.S. and Canada only.

Free Gift Certificate

Name: _____

Address: _____

City: _____ State/Province: _____ Zip/Postal Code: _____

Mail this certificate, one proof-of-purchase and a check or money order for postage and handling to: HARLEQUIN FREE GIFT OFFER 1997. In the U.S.: 3010 Walden Avenue, P.O. Box 9071, Buffalo NY 14269-9057. In Canada: P.O. Box 604, Fort Erie, Ontario L2Z 5X3.

FREE GIFT OFFER   084-KEZ
ONE PROOF-OF-PURCHASE
To collect your fabulous FREE GIFT, a cubic zirconia pendant, you must include this original proof-of-purchase for each gift with the properly completed Free Gift Certificate.

084-KEZ